THE BARCODE REBELLION

CAROLINE COONEY
Freeze Tag

DIANE HOH
The Accident

RODMAN PHILBRICK AND LYNN HARTNETT
Abduction

CHRISTOPHER PIKE
Weekend

R. L. STINE
The Boyfriend

R. L. STINE
Hit and Run

CAROLINE COONEY
Twins

DIANE HOH
Nightmare Hall: The Silent Scream

CHRISTOPHER PIKE
Slumber Party

TONYA PINES, EDITOR
Thirteen

R. L. STINE
The Girlfriend

SUZANNE WEYN
The Bar Code Tattoo

THE BARCODE REBELLION

SUZANNE WEYN

SCHOLASTIC INC.

New York Toronto London Auckland Sydney
Mexico City New Delhi Hong Kong Buenos Aires

If you purchased this book without a cover, you should be aware that this book is stolen property. It was reported as "unsold and destroyed" to the publisher, and neither the author nor the publisher has received any payment for this "stripped book."

No part of this publication may be reproduced, stored in a retrieval system, or transmitted in any form or by any means, electronic, mechanical, photocopying, recording, or otherwise, without written permission of the publisher. For information regarding permission, write to Scholastic Inc., Attention: Permissions Department, 557 Broadway, New York, NY 10012.

ISBN-13: 978-0-439-80385-4
ISBN-10: 0-439-80385-3

Text copyright © 2006 by Suzanne Weyn. All rights reserved. Published by Scholastic Inc. SCHOLASTIC, POINT, and associated logos are trademarks and/or registered trademarks of Scholastic Inc.

12 11 10 9 8 7 6 5 4 3 2 1 7 8 9 10 11 12/0

Printed in the U.S.A. 01

First printing, August 2006

ACKNOWLEDGMENTS

Suzanne Weyn thanks and deeply appreciates these people for sharing with her their great ideas, insights, and most especially their interest in this book, this story so close to her heart: Tisha Hamilton, Greg Holch, David Levithan, Robert Maloney, David M. Young (the real one), Karen Weise, and Ted Weyn. (Thanks, Dad, for the recommended related readings.)

Every separate sin and sorrow which wore the hearts of king and people was foreknown by her, proclaimed by her. But though event after event showed her predictions true, her people continued to disregard her warnings, and to treat her as a vain enthusiast.

Louisa Menzies
***Lives of the Greek Heroines* (1880)**

PRELUDE

A PUBLIC SERVICE ANNOUNCEMENT
FROM GLOBAL-1
October 13, 2025

Kayla Reed spoke directly into the camera as it closed in on her earnest face.

"When I turned seventeen, I couldn't wait to get my bar code tattooed to my wrist. It was my way of showing I wanted to become an active, responsible member of society. It was the first thing I set out to do on the morning of my birthday . . . but as it turned out, I turned seventeen on the same morning that Gene Drake, the Global-1 agent who was doing the tattooing, went insane and opened fire on the crowd. He might have killed many people if the Global-1 police hadn't been able to take him down so efficiently."

She paused, letting the full horror of the scene fully impress itself on the minds of her viewers. She quivered with emotion but regained her composure. "The event left me extremely upset and confused," she continued. "It caused me to do things I now regret. Many months later my Global-1–assigned therapeutic counselor has explained how this violence affected me. I was deeply traumatized by the shooting. In my fragile state I was easily brainwashed by members of Decode, the group dedicated to wiping out the bar code tattoo. I even joined the bar code resistance myself." She cast her eyes downward in a show of deep shame and remorse.

When she looked up again, it was as though she had been reborn with a blissful inner joy. Her lovely face glowed with the zeal of one who has come into a new and glorious light of realization. "My life is so much better now that I've seen the advantage of being tattooed with my own personal bar code. I've rejoined society and regained my self-esteem. Those horrible days are behind me. I *love* my bar code tattoo . . . and I know now that everything is going to be all right."

The screen turned blue. Words appeared on it. Above them were the black, parallel, even lines of a bar code. A warm-voiced announcer intoned, "That was Kayla Marie Reed, former bar code resister, giving a testimony to the good things brought to you by Global-1 and the bar code tattoo. Global-1, making friends around the world! This has been a public service announcement from Global-1."

PART 1

I'm nobody! Who are you?
Are you nobody, too?
Then there's a pair of us — don't tell!
They'd banish us, you know.

"I'm Nobody! Who Are You?"
Emily Dickinson

I woke up in a Soho doorway
A policeman knew my name

"Who Are You?"
The Who

CHAPTER 1

Kayla stood just inside the side door of the deli by the Garrison train station. She was transfixed by the image on the old plasma TV playing above the counter. What she was seeing there left her speechless, too stunned to alert Mfumbe.

She stared up in total shock at the image of a face on the screen. It was one she knew better than any other — her own face.

This girl was Kayla — but not. She was meticulously groomed, from her sleek blond hairstyle down to the silver manicured nails. She wore a full face of tasteful makeup. She twinkled with sincerity.

Mfumbe was walking from the back of the store, coming toward her fast. His jacket pockets bulged with the things he'd stolen. A warning flash in his dark eyes told her they had to get out quickly.

"Hey! You there! Stop!" the man behind the counter shouted. "What's in your pockets?"

They raced out the side door, sliding and stumbling down a steep bank of rocks and dirt. The man was right behind them.

They scrambled onto the old railroad tracks, the ones closest to the Hudson River. "I'm calling the cops!" the man shouted from atop the embankment as they raced down the tracks, leaping over broken ties that had come loose and rolled to the center. The new BulleTrain lines were at their side.

A bag of chips fell from Mfumbe's pocket. They both stooped to grab it. Who knew when they'd have a chance to get food again?

"Come on! Come on!" Mfumbe urged her, stuffing the bag in his pocket. He took her hand as they continued to run, and she had to increase her speed to keep up. If they got caught, it was all over.

When they finally felt reasonably sure that no one was after them, they slowed to a walk. The October day was still pleasant and sunny. The trees around them and on the far shore of the river were ablaze with autumn color. Kayla told Mfumbe about what she'd seen on the TV.

"It was someone who *looked* like you?" he asked.

"No! It *was* me! I was talking about my old neighbor, Gene Drake. I've told you how he learned what information was in the bar code, and how it banged him out so bad he tried to destroy the tattooing laser. The Global-1 security cops shot him before he could. Only now they've twisted the story so that it sounds like *he* was the one shooting people. I was on the TV, telling everyone that I love my bar code tattoo."

She stretched out her right arm and gazed down at her wrist. There was no bar code tattoo there.

"I know it sounds crazy," she said. "But I saw it."

The Global-1 BulleTrain appeared — streaking along the magnetic track at breathtaking speed, its engine a high-pitched whisper — and was gone again in an instant. Mfumbe wiped his face of dirt and smiled, amused at the look of dismay on Kayla's face as she spit out the grime the train had sprayed.

She smiled back into his eyes, seeing herself as she must look to him — a disheveled, thinly muscular seventeen-year-old with straight light-brown chin-length hair, a wide mouth pulled into a frown, and railroad filth all over her face.

Looking back at him, she was aware of how much he'd changed over their last few months together. The black hair that he'd always kept so neatly short was now long and wild with curls. His brown skin had slowly deepened in color from all the time they'd spent outdoors in the mountains.

He reached into the pocket of his torn jeans and pulled out half a stick of peppermint gum and handed it to her. Peppermint gum was his special cure for all the trouble in the world. He'd given her some the first day they'd met, a little over a year ago. When he handed her the wrapped sweetness, it was more than gum — it was his way of reminding her of his love. It always worked its intended magic, every time.

Where did you get this? she asked, speaking from her mind directly to his mind as she turned the treasured gum in her hand.

It's my emergency half stick, he revealed, smiling with satisfaction at having surprised and pleased her. *When we get to the old warehouse at Indian Point I'm going to see if I can hook us up with a ride. I hear the clubs on the strip are still hot-wired to the underground. It sounds like you can score anything if you know who to ask. The bar code hasn't changed that.*

The warehouse was a safe haven where they'd once held their anti–bar code meetings. There had been six of them then. Now they were completely scattered.

I can't wait to get there, she told him. *But it's still miles away.*

We'll get there, he assured her, gently lifting her chin as he kissed her lips. She wrapped her arms around him and kissed him back.

As she pressed her forehead into the hollow of his shoulder, she took a moment to slow her racing, unsettled thoughts. The image she'd seen on the screen had messed with her mind in a big way.

If it was a vision of what was to come, it wouldn't be the first time a flash of future sight had come upon her, swooping in without any summoning. It had started when she was about thirteen. Now that she'd learned to cultivate the talent, the visions came to her more clearly and more frequently.

In fact, right now she was headed toward something she'd already seen herself doing in a vision months earlier. She'd envisioned Mfumbe joining her at a march on Washington long before she had even dreamed of joining the bar code resistance — before she'd even met Mfumbe.

If the broadcast image of herself was another vision, did it mean she would eventually get a bar code tattoo? Would she go on TV and encourage others to get it? What was going to happen that could *ever* compel her to make such a complete turnaround, disavowing everything she passionately believed?

The bar code was wrong. It was degrading and put government control right on your skin. It reduced you to a code. And more than that, it said that you were to be judged solely on the basis of your genetic code.

What many people hadn't known — and still weren't aware of — was that every person with the tattoo had his or her genetic history encoded in the lines of the bar code. The new world that was being created by the bar code tattoo was one where the genetically healthy were given everything, and those with genetic liabilities — inherited diseases, personality flaws, psychological disorders, or any physical weakness — could waste away.

Even the new micro-chip technologies had not had the impact on society that the bar code had. People feared having the chips embedded in their skin, but they were comfortable with tattoos and bar codes, making them more ready to accept the bar code tattoo.

Only a small group realized the implications, saw the danger. Only a few, like Kayla, had learned how the information stored there was being used.

Why would she ever go on TV and tell people to get a bar code tattoo when she knew only too well that it had the hidden power to destroy their lives?

You're thinking about what you saw on the TV again, aren't you? Mfumbe cut into her thoughts.

Yeah, she admitted.

It had taken him months to catch up to her telepathic skill. It still taxed his strength, but he had the ability. The population of resisters living in the Adirondack mountain range had all cultivated some version of telepathy.

Mfumbe believed everyone could learn to become telepathic, or at least carried the potential in their genetic suitcase of untapped abilities. He figured this telepathy was a latent power that had recently been activated by circumstances. It was what people needed to thwart the repressive measures of the corporate giant, Global-1, the only tool that gave them any chance at all. So what had been a mostly dormant ability was coming forward, like a weak, underutilized muscle that was suddenly strengthened by constant use.

Kayla wasn't sure about the theory; all she knew was that she'd grown so close to Mfumbe that communicating with him like this felt as natural as talking — even more so because it sprang from her mind, unfiltered. It wasn't something she would attempt with just anyone.

After more walking, they sat on the track ties to eat the food he'd stolen. Kayla didn't like that they were forced to steal. Before they'd left the mountains, they'd packed as much food as they could carry, but it was gone now. Cash money had been eliminated five years ago. Stores no longer accepted e-cards. The bar code tattoo was the only acceptable form of payment left. Without it, they couldn't buy anything, and they couldn't get jobs.

They opened the chips, pretzels, pack of cheese, and rolls Mfumbe had managed to pilfer. The bottle of water they split was refreshing and brought Kayla new energy.

When they were done, she took out the art supplies she had made for herself in the Adirondacks. To make a sketchbook, she'd stitched together the blank sides of political flyers that circulated through the mountains, calling for an end to the bar code tattoo. Her charcoals were left over from their campfires.

"Stand up. I want to sketch you," she said.

As Mfumbe got to his feet, he took a dog-eared paperback volume of poetry from his pack. "It's too boring to just stand here. I'll read you a poem while you work," he suggested, thumbing through the pages for a selection she might like. "Here's one just for you," he said, opening the book. "It's from the sixteenth century. 'Come live with me and be my love. . . .' "

He read on as she sketched him there, with the Hudson River and the low-lying mountains of the distant shore behind him. A flock of birds lifted from the shore and swooped in unison, flying an elaborate spiral dance before settling again.

Kayla stopped sketching a moment in order to watch them. Birds fascinated her. How did they do that, seeming to fly with one mind, each of them able to anticipate what the others would do?

As she worked, she thought of the crowds of people descending on the nation's capital at that very moment. Were they like the flocks of birds, moving with one mind, using the telepathy so many of them had developed to fight Global-1 and the bar code tattoo?

She wanted desperately to believe that this would work, that their telepathy gave them the power to fight Global-1.

Still — the forces against them were powerful.

THE HILLS ARE ALIVE — WITH THE DISSIDENT SOUNDS OF RESISTANCE

By Nedra Harris

Lake Placid, NY. October 13, 2025 — Ever since May 19, 2025, when the Senate approved President Loudon Waters's bill requiring all citizens to be tattooed with their personal bar code on their seventeenth birthday, some people have resisted. What were once random pockets of the disenfranchised and malcontent, oddballs obsessed with a host of wild conspiracy theories, soon mushroomed to a population explosion of bar code tattoo resisters in the Adirondack Mountains.

These groups of resisters are highly distinct from one another. Indeed, a dislike of the bar code is all that links some of them. One resistance group sits in a field for days at a time, chanting, hoping to attract help from outer space. Others of these lunatic fringe groups, like the one headed by the Cherokee shaman Eutonah Clearwater, spend their days cultivating so-called psychic abilities in the misbegotten belief that only in this way can they "transcend" the "degrading and dehumanizing effects of the bar code."

Other groups take a less peaceful approach. A resistance group calling its members Drakians (after Gene Drake, the disgruntled bar code tattoo agent who opened fire on a line of citizens waiting to be tattooed in a Global-1 Postal Office on April 16, 2025) advocates violent resistance to the bar code and is considered dangerous. They are suspected of having taken refuge in the mountains, although lately their members have not been seen in the area, causing authorities to suspect they have moved their headquarters to another location.

Those in the resistance who remain untattooed are all in violation of the May 2025 tattoo law. Beyond that, many have a history of trouble with the law. A raid of the mountains in August 2025 yielded a number of wanted criminals, among them Kayla Marie Reed, 17, a fugitive criminal and member of Ms. Clearwater's group. She was identified during a raid on Whiteface Mountain but initially evaded capture. Ms. Reed was wanted by police on charges of arson, second-degree murder, evading arrest, fleeing the scene of an accident, and aggravated assault of a government agent.

It is believed that Ms. Reed set fire to her

own Yorktown, NY, home after a dispute with her mother, Ashley Reed, 43, on May 22, 2025. The fire resulted in the death of Mrs. Reed. Ms. Reed then fled police. She later was involved in a high-speed police chase and subsequent crash resulting in the deaths of Mava and Toz Alan, her companions. Ms. Reed fled authorities until a month later, when an anonymous tip revealed she was hiding in the woods of northern upstate New York with former classmate Mfumbe Taylor. Mr. Taylor, student president of the National Honor Society at Oprah Winfrey High School, achieved some fame in 2024 as the champion of the first ever Virtual Global Teen *Jeopardy!*

Ms. Reed, in the company of Mr. Taylor, was not spotted again until the August raid. Mr. Taylor and Ms. Reed both escaped capture by assaulting an agent of Tattoo Generation, the youth group advocating Tattoo Pride that is underwritten by Global-1. Agent Zekeal Morrelle was found unconscious and described how Mr. Taylor and Ms. Reed had brutally attacked him. Though the agent is recovering, a violent blow to his head caused a blood clot that has permanently blinded him in one eye. It was only later that Ms. Reed turned herself in and began her rehabilitation.

With the bar code resistance attracting these types of people to our beautiful mountains, this is no less than a contagion threatening the pristine beauty of the Adirondacks. No longer are the mountains safe for hikers and campers. The very reputation of the Adirondacks is at stake. Those who have long loved this area should call for a careful monitoring of this activity and the forced expulsion of these dangerous groups.

CHAPTER 2

The cramped hydrogen-powered two-seater hummed along the Superlink toward Baltimore with soundless ease. In the tiny baggage space in back, Kayla squirmed to relieve the numbness that had settled into one of her legs.

She was thinking about a black-capped chickadee.

On the day Mfumbe and she had decided to leave their safe, peaceful Adirondack cabin, their cat, Lee, had killed the small black-and-white bird. Some convergence of pity, compassion, and hope had compelled her to cradle it in her hands and attempt to channel her life force into its body. In her mind's eye she saw her inner energy as a blue stream running through her palms and into the dead bird.

The effort had drained her. But she had kept on focusing.

After some time, the bird had quivered almost imperceptibly in her grasp. Astounded by her own power, she'd slowly uncupped her hands and gazed down, marveling at the rise and fall of its downy chest.

Seconds later, it had flown to the nearest branch.

Immediately, she'd known that she was strong enough to stop hiding. She agreed to come back and lend her energy to what she believed in.

Thinking of the bird reminded her of a song. It was from the turn of the century and she'd always liked it. "I'm like a bird, I only fly away," she began to sing quietly.

The buzz-cut driver of the car glanced back at her irritably. When he twisted his thick neck, the bar code tattoo permanently imprinted at the base of his head did a snakelike undulation.

The back-of-the-neck placement had become very hip. "The two of you are breathing too loud!" he screamed. They'd realized, too late, that the driver of the ride they'd picked up at Indian Point was some kind of psycho.

"Listen, maybe we should get out at that Super Eatery up ahead," Kayla suggested. She couldn't take another second of this maniac.

Good call, Mfumbe agreed telepathically.

The driver swung the car wildly onto the turnoff to the orange-roofed Super Eatery. Kayla winced as she set her foot outside the car; the blister on her left heel burned with pain. It had developed when they were right outside Peekskill. She'd barely hobbled into the warehouse before Mfumbe found them this ride. *I can hardly walk,* she told Mfumbe. *Let's go inside so I can get some toilet paper to put in my sneaker to cushion this blister.*

Inside, the overly air-conditioned lobby was

bustling with lunchtime business. On a newsstand, *The Baltimore Sun* proclaimed the big news story of the day in bold letters: **DISSENTERS DESCEND ON CAPITAL TO PROTEST BAR CODE — POLICE PREPARED FOR ANY TROUBLE.**

Kayla hurried to the bathroom to attend to her painful blister. Leaning against a sink, she gingerly peeled off the blood-soaked heel of her sock.

"Ouch," a female voice commiserated.

Kayla looked up sharply into the face of a very elderly dark-skinned woman with wild, wiry white hair. The woman's eyes scanned Kayla's exposed skin and settled on her wrist. "No code, I see. Going to the march?" she asked.

Although it was too late, Kayla impulsively pulled her arm away. Knowing who to trust wasn't easy these days.

"It's all right, dear," the woman assured her, extending her own uncoded wrist. "I'm going, too. Many years ago I walked for my people with Dr. King. This time I'm walking with the senior citizens who are dying because of this damn code. You know, if a person over eighty-five goes into a hospital with one of these bar code things on, that person does not come out. When they scan the code it must send them a message that says TOO OLD!"

"Does this remind you of when you walked with Martin Luther King?" Kayla asked, awed to meet someone who had participated in such an amazing piece of history.

"In some ways," the woman answered. "Of course, the city wasn't surrounded by that awful blast wall back then, but it was a march for human dignity, like this march."

"Do you think we'll make a difference?" Kayla asked hopefully.

The woman sighed. "These things don't come easy. All we can do is keep trying." She patted Kayla's shoulder. "I'd invite you to ride down with us but our little compact seniormobile is packed to capacity." She rummaged in her purse and pulled out a silverpatch Band-Aid. "Here. It will heal that blister in a snap."

"Thanks," Kayla said, taking the Band-Aid from her. She washed the blister with a paper towel the woman handed her. How many fights had this woman seen? Yet she was still strong. Still fighting. Kayla wondered if a person ever got to stop fighting.

"Good luck. Maybe I'll see you there," Kayla said as she slipped back into her sneaker.

Ready or not, she was newly determined to go.

DISSENTERS DESCEND ON CAPITAL TO PROTEST BAR CODE — POLICE PREPARED FOR ANY TROUBLE

Washington, DC. October 14, 2025— Under the umbrella of the anti–bar coding organization known as Decode, various groups opposed to the government's bar code tattoo bill of May 2025 have mobilized against the policy signed into law by President Loudon Waters. Decode is headed by the former junior senator from Massachusetts, David Young, who resigned his Senate seat earlier this year in protest over the bill. Young is the son of the former head of the Domestic Affairs Committee, retired Senator Ambrose Young.

David Young is calling for President Loudon Waters to resign, claiming that Waters is in the employ of the giant multinational corporation Global-1, acting exclusively in that corporation's best interests. Among other allegations, Mr. Young claims that Global-1 spent billions of dollars above the legal campaign spending cap, including money to bribe members of his opponent's campaign and to pay hackers to tamper with computerized voting machines.

Although Global-1 has successfully bid on many government contracts over the course of the past fifteen years, it remains a privately held corporation. If Senator Young's claims are found to be true, this could warrant President Waters's impeachment. The President, however, has stated that he has no formal affiliation with Global-1 other than that of "affable partners committed to an efficient government."

Hundreds if not thousands of protesters will participate in the march, which will culminate in a gathering outside the White House. There, it is rumored, Senator Young will challenge the President to come out and hear the demands of the people to end mandatory bar code tattooing. Senator Young has expressed the view that beyond being a violation of constitutional privacy guarantees, there is more to the bar code tattoo than has been revealed to the public. In announcing the march, he said, "I challenge President Waters to stop denying that other information is stored in the bar code. He *must* come clean with the American people." Informed sources say that Senator Young will launch charges that each citizen's genetic code is contained within the bars of the bar code tattoo and that this information is being used by banks, health-care providers, insurance companies, corporate human resources departments, and in a host of other venues in ways that are both discriminatory and unconstitutional.

DC police have stated that they will not tolerate even the slightest threat of violence from protesters and have constructed portable jailing facilities to accommodate mass arrests should they become necessary. The police will not close off the white blast walls that surround the city, originally constructed to protect against terrorist attack. "This is still a free country," said Global-1 Chief of Police Dean White. "All we ask is that folks obey the law." Chief White said that he had attempted to communicate with the Secret Service to coordinate peacekeeping efforts but was still awaiting a reply.

CHAPTER 3

The closer they got to DC, the more people they saw headed in the same direction. The sides of the Superlink were crowded with pedestrians. The highway itself was jammed with slow-moving traffic.

Kayla was elated by the sights around her — a procession of free people without bar codes, all technically lawbreakers by virtue of their uncoded status, but out in the open, unafraid. The silverpatch was healing Kayla's foot, and her enthusiasm at being part of this movement of like-minded people made her footsteps light with excitement.

As they walked, Mfumbe even managed to allay some of her anxiety over what she'd seen on TV. *It was a digital computer simulation,* he suggested logically as the high white blast walls surrounding the capital came into view. *They probably filmed someone else who looked like you and merged her digitally with your yearbook picture. Since your house burned down, that's the only picture they've got.*

It made sense. It explained why the smiling,

repentant girl was so old-Kayla. *But why would they use my picture?* she questioned. *Why me?*

Who do you know who hates you and is also the national spokesperson for Tattoo Gen? he challenged her to recall.

Her eyes widened as the realization dawned. Nedra Harris! Of course!

I bet she orchestrated it to mess with your head, discredit you in the resistance, and maybe even trick you into thinking they're not looking for you anymore, he added.

All that might have upset her if it had not been so much better than the alternatives that had been running through her head. It meant she *wasn't* seeing a vision of the future in which she betrayed everything she believed in. It also discredited her other, even more terrifying fear — that the schizophrenia that ran in her family was manifesting itself in the form of this chillingly paranoid hallucination.

They were just inside the blast walls when a sleek fighter jet streaked by. It was flying low. She'd never seen one like it, yet it seemed familiar somehow.

A male voice came into her head, but it didn't belong to Mfumbe. *It's a robot jet,* the voice said. *It's taking surveillance photos of the protesters.* Kayla looked at a nearby group gazing up at the jet. Someone in that group had spoken to them all. Learning which telepathic speakers to block and which to receive was going to be tricky here in the middle of such a largely telepathic crowd.

When the jet had passed, they resumed their walk toward the city. She realized where she'd seen the jet before — in one of her visions. She'd foreseen this entire event.

Kayla stood outside the White House at dusk in a crowd of approximately a thousand other protesters. It had been the most inspiring, thrilling day of her life.

They had been fired on by a jet as they approached the walls, but no one had been seriously hurt. News reports said that the Secret Service claimed the release of ammunition had been a mistake in the programming of the robot craft, though the protesters believed it had been an attempt to scare them off.

In a speech at the Lincoln Memorial later that afternoon, David Young, a charismatic man in his late thirties, had told the protesters to focus on a world where people moved freely and were unafraid. He urged them to envision a society of equality and justice where all were valued, regardless of their genetic code. "We will not use violence to achieve our end," he continued, "but we can use the strength and energy of our minds to change our world."

Now they stood outside the White House waiting for David Young to emerge with Loudon Waters in tow. Finally, they were going to force their so-called President to give them some straight answers.

"Hey! Over here!" Kayla and Mfumbe turned toward the familiar voice that had called to them. A short, heavy-set guy with dyed neon orange hair waved to them. August Sanchez was maneuvering his way through the crowd that separated them. His burly frame barreled through with the determination of a linebacker.

"I thought you'd decided not to come, man," Mfumbe said, gripping August's arm in delighted solidarity.

"You guys shamed me into it," August replied, smiling. "And I was getting bored spending all day in a field trying to contact alien life-forms with my mind. It seemed like a good idea at first but, I mean, come on. My brain was starting to hurt. You guys were only gone half a day when I started to miss you. I tried to catch up, but you two move fast."

"We'd have waited for you if we had known," Kayla said as she hugged August. He was their friend from high school and part of their original resistance group. Like them, he'd wound up in the Adirondack Mountains, but he had joined a group that hoped to contact outer space with their thoughts. Although it had seemed bizarre to Kayla, the people involved were sympathetic to the resistance. "Just before I left, I got a letter from Allyson," he added, pulling an envelope from his back pocket.

"Postman?" Mfumbe asked. Postmen, who were both men and women, secretly passed mail from one person to the next until it reached its intended recipient. It was an act of resistance, a way of circumventing e-mail that could be read by the prying electronic eyes of Global-1 and bypassing phones, which were also known to be monitored. The Postmen's skill at tracking people was quickly becoming legendary.

It was said that Postmen never gave up. They simply asked if anyone had seen or even heard of the intended recipient of the letter. Then they either passed the letter on or asked some more, and tracked and tracked until their letters were delivered. They performed this task with a dogged determination resembling religious fervor.

August nodded, unfolding the handwritten letter. Allyson was another one of their group, their science whiz, always rational and sensible. Kayla thought of her now in her loose, flowing clothing, her blond curls like a halo around her face. For Allyson, not getting the bar code tattoo would have meant passing up a huge scholarship that she needed. It was her dream to study genetics at Harvard, and so, in the end, she'd gotten the tattoo.

"How is she?" Kayla asked.

"Here. Read it yourself." He handed her the letter, and once again Kayla saw the twisted, angry scar on his wrist where he'd scorched off the bar code he'd allowed them to tattoo on him in a moment of hopeless despair.

August 20, 2025

Hey Augie!

I hope a Postman can find you with this letter. I'm sending it this way because your handwritten letter found its way to me and I figure you don't have a computer or would rather not use it. I hear Postmen are very effective in finding people; their skill at it is said to be really final level.

I sure do miss you and Kayla and Mfumbe. I almost miss Zeke. Still can't believe he was working for Tattoo Gen. Don't miss Nedra, I must admit. She was probably the one who convinced him to turn against the cause.

I wonder if Kayla and Mfumbe are mad at us for getting tattooed. At least you had the guts to burn your tattoo off. I'm stuck with mine until I graduate, and even then I don't know if I'll be able to stand the pain.

Speaking of graduating, guess where I am? Not Harvard as I'd planned. I'm in Pasadena, California, at the California Institute of Technology, Caltech! I was all set to go to Harvard when I got this great opportunity to study with a professor named Dr. Gold, who studied with Richard Feynman when he taught at Caltech. (Gold was a sixteen-year-old budding genius at the time.) Feynman was a Nobel Prize winner in physics and he was talking about nanotechnology — the extreme miniaturization of machinery — as far back as 1959!

Gold has also worked with Ian Wilmut, who headed the team that cloned Dolly the sheep last century. He also worked in the same lab with James Thomson, who practically invented stem cell research, and with Patrick Brown, who invented the first DNA microarray, one of the most powerful tools in genetic research.

Caltech is the center for robotic research in the country right now, and Gold is doing amazing work on disassembling viruses using nanotechnology. In other words, he's using molecular-size robots to get into the bloodstream and literally take a virus apart. This work started at the beginning of the century, but Gold has built a better nanobot. Not only could it wipe out all viral diseases in the next five years, it has the potential to increase the human life-span to about 170, 50 years longer than our current average of 120.

Anyway! Don't get me started, as they used to say. I'm working day and night on the research and loving every second of it. I feel that I sold out by getting the bar code tattoo, but this door would have been closed to me if I hadn't, and there's potential here to do so much good. It's funny — I was determined to study genetics, but this work with nanotechnology is so fascinating and includes genetic medicine. I just can't decide where to specialize.

I hope you are well and that you find aliens soon. To quote Shakespeare's *Hamlet*, "There are more things in heaven and earth, Horatio/Than are dreamt of in your philosophy." In other words, who knows? Anything's possible. I love you for trying.

Stay hopeful and brave,

Allyson

CHAPTER 4

"I miss Allyson, too," Kayla said, handing the letter back to August.

She, Mfumbe, and August continued to wait for David Young to come out with Loudon Waters. She felt nervous despite the fact that she'd had a vision of the event. In it, she'd seen David Young smiling as he walked out behind an angry-looking, defeated President about to announce his resignation.

In the next second, they appeared, like a rerun of a movie she'd already seen. People around her grew hoarse with cheering. Others beamed joyfully as emotional tears streamed down their faces. All around her, protesters hugged friends as well as strangers. Mfumbe and August slapped their palms together in the air. Mfumbe turned and hugged Kayla. This was the moment they'd dreamed of!

Kayla was cheering along with the others when she became aware of a low whine. She swatted the air, thinking it was a mosquito. Mfumbe's face became puzzled and he checked around, then up. His expression changed from confusion to alarm as he pointed skyward.

In V formation, a squad of sleek white jets, identical to the robot jet that had fired on them earlier, flew over the White House and toward the crowd.

They were coming lower.

Too low.

An anxious murmur swept through the crowd.

A man broke loose from the protesters and dashed across the street. As others witnessed his panic, they began to run.

Kayla was aware of a rushing telepathic buzz of frantic communication filling her mind. *What's that?They'regoingtoattack.No.It'sjustsurveillance. No,it'snot.They'retoolow!They'reattackingus!*

The jets broke formation, flying off in different directions. "Let's get out of here!" August yelled, running. Mfumbe grabbed Kayla's hand, holding tight, and they began to run in the same direction as August.

Somewhere, something exploded, the boom reverberating. Kayla felt the vibration in her bones. She and Mfumbe moved closer together, stunned, as all around them people began shouting and yelling.

Global-1 cruisers appeared, blocking the entrances to side streets. Kayla coughed hard. Mfumbe's hand was over his mouth and he seemed to be choking. Several yards away, August staggered forward, gasping for breath. *Some kind of crowd control gas,* she heard Mfumbe say. *We've got to get out of here!*

Hot tears stung her eyes as they stumbled through the escaping crowd. Someone pushed Mfumbe but Kayla clutched his shirt, keeping him from toppling over.

She was still steadying him when a wave of nausea hit her. It was something in the gas.

She released his shirt and stumbled several steps away from him. Clutching her stomach, she began to vomit uncontrollably.

Heavy footsteps came up behind her. As she lifted her head to see who it was, something smashed down hard across her shoulders with incredible force. She was knocked down — and almost knocked out.

Through slitted eyes she was aware of red spinning lights. A man's voice boomed through an address system, bellowing commands. "DEPOSIT ALL CELL PHONES IN THE BINS PROVIDED. ANY PHONES NOT VOLUNTARILY SURRENDERED WILL BE FORCIBLY TAKEN. PROCEED IN AN ORDERLY FASHION AS INSTRUCTED BY THE GLOBAL-1 OFFICER NEAREST YOU."

The pain in her back was terrible. When she tried to push herself up, she was forced back to the ground by its searing ferocity.

"Quick! Quick!" someone whispered nearby. A woman's voice. "Take her to the truck."

Strong hands grasped her firmly by the upper arms.

A high whine of animal pain flew from her parched lips when they moved her. Her legs were lifted off the ground and she was spirited away across the dark street, too weak to resist.

CHAPTER 5

Kayla dreamed she was walking through a burning building. It was her high school. Smoke blackened the hallways. She pulled off her T-shirt and soaked it in the water fountain before holding the cloth over her nose and mouth. Inside each classroom, flames blazed out of control, engulfing desks, books, and posters like a ravenous monster.

Through the blinding smoke, a soot-blackened woman floated toward her, her feet dangling just above the ground. Her hair was aflame. It blazed around her head, a fiery halo.

Kayla sucked in a sharp breath of smoke-filled air as she realized who the woman was. The fiery, ephemeral figure was her dead mother. "Kayl-l-la," she intoned, her voice trilling as if some mechanism within it had become stuck on the *l*, a tinny, metallic sound. Her mother's voice *had* sounded like that, occasionally stalling on a consonant sound. Why had she never noticed it before?

Paralyzed with shock, Kayla was unable to react as the haunting vision of her mother approached. "Kayl-l-l . . ." Her mother's face twisted into a grimace of frustration as though the effort of speaking was defeating her. And then, with a sudden burst of determination, she began to scream. "You don't know! You don't know! You don't know! You don't —"

Still screaming, Ashley Reed reached out and touched Kayla's hair. It, too, burst into jets of white-hot fire.

"No!" Kayla shrieked, shielding her face with her hands. She raised her arms high as the fire jumped from her head and raced along her arms to her fingertips. "No!"

Her body began to gyrate uncontrollably, then lifted into the air and began banging off the walls.

"Wake up!" a woman commanded firmly as she shook Kayla's shoulders.

Kayla's eyes snapped open. She was in a dark place, on a hard floor. Her first response was to run. She scrambled to her feet, but a hand caught her firmly by the wrist. Kayla yanked it away.

The pain in her back drove her to her knees. Instantly, the other person was by her side. A high beam microlight snapped on, illuminating a woman's face. "Do you remember me?"

"Katie." Kayla recalled the long-haul trucker who had once given her a lift to the Superlink. It had been on the night she'd escaped from the hospital where they had wanted to bar-code her.

During the ride they'd discussed the bar code tattoo. There was cancer in Katie's family, a fact that would stop her from getting a job, health insurance, a mortgage, and so much else the moment anyone scanned her tattoo. So she'd chosen not to get one. Before they parted company, Katie had given Kayla her last fake bar code tattoo. It had served Kayla well until it had been smeared off by first-aid cream.

"No one has called me Katie in the last six months," the woman said. "I've changed my name since we last met. I started to go by my e-name, Medusa, after I had a little trouble with the law. It makes it harder to track me, and I kind of like it better anyway. It's scary."

"Wasn't Medusa thc snake-headed Gorgon woman?" Kayla recalled, remembering her ancient Greek mythology. "People turned to stone if they looked at her face. You're right — it *is* scary. Who are you trying to scare?"

"Global-1. Those Tattoo Gen creeps. Anyone who's on my trail."

"What kind of trouble are you in?" Kayla asked.

"I started transporting bar code tattoo resisters to Canada illegally. It's nearly impossible to cross the border these days, but I found ways. I took a lot of old people who believed they were going to be killed in the hospital."

Kayla recalled a couple, the Alans, who had been fleeing to Canada to join their physician daughter, Sarah, there. They'd helped Kayla before G-1 police had tracked them down — and they'd died in a car crash trying to escape. She also remembered the woman she'd met in the Super Eatery who was marching with senior citizens against the bar code tattoo. Kayla hoped she was all right.

"I got caught crossing the border one night and had to make a run for it," Katie-Medusa went on. "After that, I was wanted by the G-1 cops, so it seemed better to change my name. The problem was that no one liked saying Medusa so it got shortened to Dusa. You might as well call me that now."

"How did you find me?"

"I've been following your story in the news. I recognized you lying there on Pennsylvania Avenue and figured I'd better pick you up before the G-1 cops did. We're in the trailer of my rig, parked in an underground garage just outside Georgetown."

"Did you see Mfumbe?" she asked. "August?"

"Friends of yours?" Dusa inquired. Kayla nodded. "You were alone. The G-1 cops would have scooped you up eventually, but lucky for you they were still a ways off grabbing other people they'd gassed and clubbed. Maybe they weren't sure if you were seventeen or not. If you were sixteen, they might have been in trouble for clobbering you because you're not in violation of the law yet. They couldn't have hauled you in and charged you with not having a bar code." She shrugged uncertainly. "They might still have charged you with being a public nuisance or jaywalking or something. Who knows what they'll come up with?"

"Why didn't they get you?"

Dusa smiled bitterly. "Drakians know better. Did you really think Global-1 was going to lie down and die because a thousand idealists demanded that their front man, their former corporate chief, Loudon Waters, should resign? They've moved mountains, spent billions, to get that guy into office. Did anyone really think they'd care what the people in this country wanted?"

"We did. *I* did, anyway," Kayla admitted, suddenly feeling foolish and naive.

"Come on," Dusa scoffed. "We were prepared for this. We realize what Global-1 is like, how they operate. We had a stock of gas masks, for one thing. We kept away until the trouble started, like we knew it would, and then we came out to see how many we could help."

"Gene Drake was my neighbor," she told Dusa.

"Are you kidding?" Dusa asked, impressed. "What was he like?"

"Honestly," Kayla replied, "he was a weird guy. He smoked these Chinese cigarettes, which I always thought was strange." Nobody in America smoked anymore, which was why he had to buy imported cigarettes. "And he had a banged-out way of yelling at his little brown terrier, even though he played ball with him in his front yard for more than an hour every day."

"I've heard that he was kind of odd," Dusa admitted. "But what we admire about him is that he acted. He learned that Global-1 was taking genetic histories from the blood samples they collect when they give a bar code, so he refused to do more codes. He ripped the laser machine right off its base . . . and they killed him for it. He's the first martyr for the resistance."

"But I've read that Drakians believe in violence and are dangerous," Kayla said.

"Propaganda. Not true," Dusa said firmly. "We act, but we don't carry weapons. We're for freedom and life, not against it."

Kayla pushed herself forward onto her hands and knees and slowly straightened to her feet. The pain was excruciating. "They whacked you good," Dusa commented. "Your fingers are moving, right?"

Kayla wiggled them and nodded. "I have to find Mfumbe. Would you just let me try something?"

"Sure."

Kayla shut her eyes. *It's Kayla. I'm okay. Where are you, Mfumbe?*

She relaxed and opened her mind to a receptive state. Instantly, she was flooded with the whispering chatter she'd heard earlier in the day. Hundreds of messages in different voices, even different languages, words tumbling over one another. *WhereareI'mokayI'm hurtwhere areyouIdon't knowreallyscared not sureareyouokayhurtfeelsick-*

come find me scaredhurt feelsick don'tworry-scared . . .

She let out a cry of anguished frustration as her eyes opened. "It's no use. I have to go look for him." Taking a step toward the door, she cringed again from the pain in her back.

"Don't worry, this time I'm not going to just send you on your way," Dusa said. "It's nearly dawn. I have to do something, and I want you to come with me. Then we'll look for your friend with the odd name."

"His great-great-times-ten grandfather was from an area that's now called Mfumbe in Zambia, in Africa," Kayla offered. "That's where his name comes from."

"Okay. Makes sense." Dusa tossed Kayla a protein bar for breakfast. "I guess it's important to know who your ancestors were, now more than ever before. Don't worry. We'll find him."

She and Kayla walked to the back of the tractor trailer. Dusa opened the back doors and leaped lightly to the ground. Extending her hand, she helped Kayla, who was moving more slowly, to descend. Inside the garage, men and women were sleeping on tattered rugs and in old sleeping bags. Dusa nudged one of the sleeping men with the scuffed, scarred toe of her boot. "So, Nate, are we going to do this thing or are you going to sleep all day?" she demanded as he came awake. "I picked up the box of fakes last night."

Nate yawned and stretched. He was only in his twenties, shaved bald, with very dark skin and the physique of a weight lifter.

Kayla had seen him before. He was one of the two roommates who had shared the house next door to hers with Gene Drake. She spotted the other roommate, a young Asian man, still asleep on a blanket nearby.

Like Gene Drake, they'd worked down at the Global-1 Post Office. After the U.S. Postal Service had gone bankrupt, Global-1 had taken over the buildings and converted them into bar code tattoo centers. The last time she'd seen either of them was right after Gene Drake's death. Global-1 police had been taking them out of their ransacked house in handcuffs as she watched from her darkened bedroom window.

"Hey, look who's here, Francis!" Nate said to the second roommate who yawned and stretched to a waking state. "It's our old neighbor — the foxy girl from next door."

Kayla had never even spoken to him and was surprised that he recognized her, let alone had noticed her looks.

Francis rolled over, sat up, and rubbed his eyes. "Do you mean the one we always thought was so sexy?" he asked.

"Yeah. She's right there!" Nate said, pointing at Kayla.

Francis squinted at Kayla and then pulled on a

pair of wire-frame glasses. "She's cute — but, Nate, that's not her."

People were coming awake all around them, disturbed by their conversation. Someone turned on a small portable TV set tuned to the news. "Our neighbor had long hair with a blue streak in it," Francis continued. "She was always kind of . . . put together."

Kayla was becoming irritated at being spoken about as if she weren't there.

"There she is!" Francis continued, pointing to the portable TV. "What are the chances of that? She's on the TV just when we're talking about her."

It was the public service announcement again. They remembered the old Kayla — and that was who they were seeing on the TV. The clean-scrubbed Kayla smiled into the camera. "I love my bar code tattoo, and I know that everything is going to be all right," she gushed.

"She's gone over to the dark side!" Francis cried indignantly. "I'd like to wring her perky little neck!"

"Well, here's your chance," Nate said, pointing at Kayla. "Like I've been telling you — she's standing right over there."

Every newly awakened eye in the dimly lit garage was now focused on Kayla. "I don't know what that's about," she insisted, holding out her right wrist to show she wore no bar code.

Dusa came alongside and brusquely rubbed the place where the bar code might have been. "No makeup over it, no patch," she reported to the others. Carefully, she bent Kayla's head forward to check the back of her neck. "Nothing," she said.

Francis stood up and swaggered up to them, leering at Kayla. "I'll have to check the rest of her."

"You're not checking anything," Dusa scoffed. "The bar code tattoo has to be easy to see when a person is fully clothed. If you can't see it, she doesn't have it."

"Then who's the babe on the TV?" he asked.

Dusa looked to Kayla for an explanation. "Do you have a sister? A twin?"

Kayla shook her head. "No brother or sister at all. Mfumbe thinks it's a digital fake up meant to make me look like I've given up the fight, or even to trick me into getting caught."

"Makes sense," Dusa conceded, and the others nodded in agreement.

"I've seen that ad before," Nate recalled. "In it you say you were there the day they shot Gene. Did you see him get killed?" A murmur of excitement ran through the group. Kayla realized that Gene Drake had taken on heroic status in the eyes of these people; even Nate and Francis, who knew differently, appeared swept up in it. They looked at her now like someone who'd had direct contact with a saint.

"I was still outside the post office," she admitted. "But I heard the shots. I saw the blood hit the window. In the ad they have me saying the event traumatized me. It did, but not in the way they meant. It *stopped* me from getting the bar code that day and made me think. What was so awful about the tattoo that it made Gene do what he did? What did he know?"

"Gene Drake gave his life so you could be free!" a woman in the group shouted. Her words were followed by cheers from the others.

"What did Gene find in the bar code?" Kayla asked Nate. Gene had told her that in his training to be a bar code tattoo provider he'd befriended someone who'd learned the password to access Global-1's bar code database. Together, he and the friend were going to hack into the Global-1 system. She'd always assumed the two of them had been successful and what they discovered had driven Gene to rip the machine from its base and hurl it at the wall — the act of defiance that had cost him his life.

"Was that when he learned that everyone's genetic history was in there?" she asked. "Was that it?"

Anxious, darting glances were exchanged between Francis, Dusa, and Nate. "We think he found something even worse than that," Nate told her. "A lot worse."

BIGGEST CRIMINAL ROUNDUP IN U.S. HISTORY — POLICE INSIST THOSE NOT BAR-CODED ARE IN VIOLATION OF LAW

Washington, DC. October 15, 2025 — "This is not just some law a citizen can choose to disregard," insisted Global-1 Chief of Police Dean White. "The law of this land states that every citizen is to be bar-coded when he or she is 17 years of age. This is not something you can have an opinion on or decide for yourself. This is the law. If you violate it, you will be arrested."

Lawyers for the American Civil Liberties Union, several of whose members were arrested last night, are claiming, however, that unwarranted force was used in making these mass arrests, and they are leveling charges of police brutality. "This dwarfs even the incident at Kent State University on May 4, 1970, when members of the Ohio National Guard fired into a crowd of Kent State University demonstrators, killing four and wounding nine Kent State students," stated ACLU lawyer Nancy Feldman. "Though there were no fatalities that we know of last night, there were serious injuries. The scale and scope of this police raid is staggering."

More than 700 protesters are believed to be in police custody, held in temporary jails set up throughout the city. The scene was chaotic as hundreds of those injured in the demonstration were given emergency care. This morning the capital is being inundated with family members of those arrested who have come looking for their loved ones. Among those taken into custody was former Senator David Young. Besides being in violation of bar code statutes, there is talk that Senator Young may be charged with coercion of President Loudon Waters. This may result in a charge of treasonous conspiracy, a charge that can result in a life sentence. "A conspiracy charge is nonsense," said former Senator Ambrose Young, David Young's father. "David simply went to talk to Loudon Waters. He persuaded him to leave the White House of his own accord. My son is not a thug who would ever force anyone to do anything against his will. Rest assured that I will aid my son in fighting this with all the considerable legal power at my command." So far, the President's spokespeople have made no comment.

CHAPTER 6

"Do you believe that Gene Drake really found something terrible in the bar code data file?" Kayla questioned Dusa as they drove together through DC in Dusa's tractor trailer.

"Francis and Nate believe it," Dusa answered. "He told them that he was working with a journalist on an exposé and he didn't want to reveal what he knew before the story came out."

"But the story never came out," Kayla reminded her.

"I don't know why. Maybe it was too hot to handle. Global-1 might have gotten to the journalist. The journalist might have been a Global-1 spy. Who knows? Francis and Nate say he knew about the genetic code stuff before this other thing. The other thing, though, was what really made him desperate."

"What could it be?" Kayla wondered aloud.

"I'm not sure I even *want* to know," Dusa said with a shiver. She pulled onto the Superlink and they drove toward Virginia.

"Where are we going?" Kayla asked after a short while. "I really need to find Mfumbe and August."

"We will. Write down their full names and a

description of them for me. I have contacts who can keep an eye out for them. We'll go look ourselves, but first we have a delivery to intercept." She handed Kayla a molded plastic cheetah mask. It reminded Kayla of an elephant mask her father had bought her once at the Bronx Zoo.

"Put it on when I tell you," Dusa instructed.

"What's going on?" Kayla asked, suddenly worried. Why were they going to need masks?

"You'll see." Dusa pulled off at the next exit. "You don't mind a little bloodshed, do you?"

The frantic questions racing through Kayla's head went unanswered. Dusa was too busy talking with Francis on the chip-size phone clipped to the collar of her T-shirt. Apparently, Francis and the others were riding right behind in the truck's trailer.

After phoning a contact with Kayla's descriptions of Mfumbe and August, Dusa turned onto a side street and pulled the tractor trailer in front of a narrow outdoor parking lot wedged between two buildings, letting the motor idle. "We've trailed this G-1 delivery guy for a week," she said to Kayla. "He goes for coffee here every morning at this time. See, there's his truck." She pointed to an unmarked compact silver truck parked in the lot.

Nate appeared from behind the truck. He wore a tiger mask and a gray sweatshirt with the hood up. Francis had already scurried into the lot and met up with Nate at the back of the silver truck.

"We wait here," Dusa advised as she slipped on a lion mask. "Put your mask on just in case someone sees us. If they report anything, let them report that a pack of wild animals did this."

"Is anyone going to be hurt?" Kayla asked.

"Hopefully not," Dusa replied tensely as she stared out the window, her attention riveted on Nate and Francis.

Kayla placed the mask over her face and watched anxiously. Dusa had said they didn't believe in violence. But this looked like trouble to her.

A light flashed near the truck. Smoke spiraled into the air as the back door of the Global-1 truck flew open and the men disappeared inside. In less than a minute, Nate and Francis raced out of the back of the truck, each of them carrying heavy black cases piled on top of one another. "Go! Go!" Dusa urged them, speaking into the phone on her collar.

From somewhere, a police siren came to life — alerted, no doubt, by the smoke.

Dusa gunned the motor. Two Global-1 cruisers swept into the street ahead of her and two came in from behind. "Put your head down, Kayla!" she shouted as she continued to drive straight for the cruisers.

Doors sprang open as the Globalofficers ran from their vehicles. With her arms over her masked face, Kayla heard the crunching and banging as Dusa knocked the cruisers aside.

A bullet smashed the mirror on the passenger side, spraying the window with clattering pebbles of safety glass. Kayla screamed, surprised and terrified.

Dusa drove for the highway at top speed. A Global-1 cruiser parked at the highway ramp tailed her onto the Superlink. "Our friends look ready," she spoke into her collar phone.

They came alongside another tractor trailer. Kayla spotted a third tractor trailer, and just ahead of them was a fourth.

"I see our target," Dusa told the guys in back. "Get ready at the doors." She was referring to three black SUVs with dark-tinted windows that were driving in front of one another in the center lane of the five-lane Superlink highway. The four big rigs came together, boxing the black SUVs in their center. Dusa and Kayla were in the lead truck.

The screaming siren of the Global-1 cruiser was still somewhere behind the truck. The SUVs trapped in the center of this enclosure had no choice but to drive at the ever-faster speed of the four trucks that had boxed them in.

Dusa honked her truck's horn and immediately the SUVs were spattered with pails of blood that were tossed from the back of her truck and from the other two on either side of the SUVs. The red blood splashed onto the windows, drenching the vehicles in deep red liquid. The SUVs braked as the truck drivers separated, heading for different exits.

The last thing Kayla saw was the Global-1 cruiser jamming its breaks to avoid hitting the blood-covered SUVs.

"We just dumped a month's worth of blood samples on the Global-1 bigwigs in those SUVs!" Dusa shouted triumphantly. "We stole them from G-1 couriers in four different locations and tossed them on the Global-1 bosses who were headed for DC. It doesn't get any better than that!"

"Oh, my God!" Kayla cried, gasping at the audacity of what had just happened.

"It's the Boston Tea Party of the twenty-first century!" Dusa shouted.

Kayla smiled broadly. It was hard not to be caught up in the victory, though they'd come scarily close to being caught and could still be caught. "Won't they trace your license plate?"

"It's a stolen plate."

"Aren't you afraid of going to jail?"

"We're outlaws, kiddo," Dusa said. "You might as well accept that. They could pull you in today for not having the code. If we're going to be outlaws anyway, we might as well not worry about it. Speaking of which —" She rapped on the back of her cab, and Nate slid open the narrow door behind her. "We have another crime to commit."

"Could you drop me off first?" Kayla requested as Dusa drove into the parking lot of a suburban mall. "I need to find Mfumbe and August."

"Like I told you, it's already being taken care

of," Dusa assured her. "There are fake-tattoo–wearing Drakians all over this city. I've already sent out word that you're looking for your friends, along with the descriptions you gave me. You'll find them faster by sitting tight than you will by trekking around on your own. Besides, your back must still hurt like hell."

"It does," Kayla admitted.

Dusa stopped on the outskirts of the mall's parking lot to allow Nate and Francis a moment to change the license plate on her truck, replacing it with another stolen one from a commercial vehicle.

Nate and Francis opened a box of fake bar code tattoos as Dusa drove, letting the fakes flutter out the back of the truck. "Blow, wind! Blow!" Dusa cheered as the fake tattoos floated on the breezes. "Take 'em like seeds and spread them all over the damn place! A free gift for free people, courtesy of the Drakians!"

Back at the garage, everyone was excited about the success of their mission. "Now there are hundreds of newly tattooed people who can't be tagged to their genetic histories," Dusa told Kayla. "Spilling their blood before it could be processed freed them!"

"But Global-1 can collect new samples," Kayla pointed out.

"True," Dusa admitted. "But it's another clog in the cog."

"What?" Kayla questioned.

Dusa laughed. "It's like throwing a wooden shoe in the machinery. It stops the wheels from turning for a while; we've messed them up for a time. More than that, it sends the message that we're not going to lie down and let them walk all over us. We won't let them define who we are or dictate how we live. There's resistance to their control, and they might as well know it."

A woman approached them. "We found Mfumbe Taylor," she reported. "He was spotted in a Waters Shed — that's what the people are calling the temporary jails that are popping up all over DC. He's in one outside the Smithsonian Institution."

"Anything on August?" Kayla asked. Dusa said there wasn't but suggested that they might find him in the jail along with Mfumbe. "Let's go," Kayla said, hurrying to the door of the garage.

"Do you feel strong enough to sit on the back of a motorcycle?" Dusa asked.

The pain in Kayla's upper back made her wince every time she made even the smallest movement, but she couldn't let it stop her.

"I love motorcycles," she said.

JAILED PROTESTERS BAR-CODED!

Washington, DC. October 15, 2025 — In a press conference early this morning, Global-1 Chief of Police Dean White defended his decision to force protesters taken into custody during yesterday's anti–bar code tattoo protest to submit to being bar-coded. "We subdued them, took a blood sample, and coded them," he explained. "This is a free country, but you don't have a choice about obeying the law. That's a must."

When asked by a reporter how those who were imprisoned and then bar-coded reacted, Chief White reported, "They were in wire cuffs, so there wasn't much they could do about it. Anyone who resisted too forcibly was given a shot of Propeace tranquilizer. After that, they didn't mind at all. No one was injured while in custody, and we were completely within our rights."

Former Senator Ambrose Young arrived in Washington with a team of lawyers. His son, Decode leader David Young, was among those forcibly bar-coded. "This is an outrage!" the senior Senator Young told reporters. "Up to this moment I have not seen eye to eye on this with my son. Now, however, I am seeing for the first time what he's been up against."

Ambrose Young was scheduled to meet with Global-1 lawyers this morning, but the latest sources report that the Global-1 lawyers did not arrive in time for the arranged meeting. The senior Senator Young was unable to have his son released on bail, though other families are having some success in getting their loved ones released if there is no prior warrant for that person's arrest.

CHAPTER 7

With bar code fakes on their wrists, Dusa and Kayla entered the quickly erected building of corrugated metal and high-tech plastics set up outside the Smithsonian Institution. "Ironic, isn't it?" Dusa said, taking off her helmet. "Hopefully, someday this jail will be *inside* the Smithsonian, just a freaky artifact of American history."

Their bar codes were scanned at the front door by a uniformed guard. Kayla held her breath nervously until he passed them through. Dusa answered her unasked question as they headed down a row of small, empty jail cells, explaining, "He was seeing a dead person's file."

Ahead of them, at the spot where the last cell stood, was a large open room lined with cots. Hundreds of people milled around, some sitting or sleeping, others pacing like caged animals. Dusa broke into a jog. Kayla was about to follow when she heard her name.

Turning quickly, she saw a tall Cherokee woman in jeans and a T-shirt. Long black hair framed a strong, weathered face with piercing dark eyes. "Eutonah!" Kayla gasped as she hurried to the cell. She'd thought her former teacher, her guide, was still in jail, but apparently Eutonah had come to the march only to be caught again.

"Kayla, listen to me," Eutonah began in her usual direct manner. "There is something you don't know. Global-1 wants you. You are more important to them than you realize — and it's not only because you're a known bar code resister."

"Why?" Kayla asked.

"I don't know that yet," Eutonah told her. "But our group intercepted an e-mail and your name was in it. Global-1 is desperate to find you. Don't let them. In fact, you shouldn't be here. Go!"

"But, Mfumbe —" Kayla began to protest. At that moment Dusa called to her, waving for her to come. Kayla turned toward her and held out her finger to gain a last moment with Eutonah, but when she turned back, the woman was no longer in the cell.

Eutonah, a shaman, could project herself through time and space. When she'd been arrested during last August's raid, she'd projected herself to Kayla in the mountains, and now she'd appeared to her again.

Global-1 was desperate to find her? Why?

Dusa was still waiting for her, and she had no time to ponder Eutonah's message. She had to find Mfumbe and get out of there. She looked for Dusa but could no longer see her. A commotion had arisen in the room as a well-dressed man of about sixty-five strode into the holding pen. It was

Ambrose Young, surrounded by a coterie of his staff and followed by reporters. The crowd of prisoners gathered around him.

Using a handheld microphone, Ambrose Young told the prisoners that he'd come to get his son but that David Young refused to leave jail until everyone who had been taken into custody was out. "And he has told me about the outrage of forced bar code tattooing that went on last night," he added. "We will get each and every one of you out of here, and you will have your day in court."

As the people stood and cheered him, Kayla wove through the throng. It seemed hopeless, the crowd was so thick. *Mfumbe, where are you?* she tried.

Walk straight back, his mental answer came. *I saw you for a second before everyone stood up.*

She didn't like the weakness she sensed in him. Something was wrong. After a few more minutes of squeezing between tightly packed bodies, she found him lying on a cot, badly battered. His right eye was purple and swollen, his lip was split. There was something about the angle of his shoulder that worried her, too. "I look good, huh?" he attempted to joke as she knelt beside his cot.

"You've looked better," she confirmed, stroking his forehead instead of kissing his injured lips.

"Here's the worst of it." He held out his right arm. A bar code tattoo was emblazoned there.

"Bastards," Kayla hissed, filled with hot rage.

Angry tears sprang to her eyes. How could they do this to him? She swept the wetness away roughly. This wasn't a time for crying.

Inside the dense crowd, someone shouted angrily. Fighting had broken out. She scanned the crowd, searching for August but not seeing him.

Dusa came alongside the cot. "Let's slip out of here in this confusion."

"I can't find August," Kayla said. "We can't leave without him."

"He's not here," Dusa reported. "One of my contacts saw your friend walking toward the Superlink this morning. It sounded like he was okay."

Mfumbe tried to pull himself up but winced in pain. He coughed harshly into his hand, and Kayla saw he'd spit up blood.

Offering her arm, Dusa helped him to hoist himself up. Kayla supported his left side, and together they pushed their way along the back wall. Dusa seemed to have an idea where she was headed, so Kayla followed her. When they reached a corner of the Waters Shed, Kayla was sure she smelled burning plastic.

Pounding her fist and kicking, Dusa forced open the spot where the walls met and the two sides came apart. Nate and Francis appeared on the other side, grinning, a blowtorch in Nate's hand. "Help us," Dusa ordered, taking the torch and shifting Mfumbe off to them. "Careful. He's hurt bad."

Kayla followed Mfumbe as Nate and Francis carried him toward Dusa's tractor trailer, parked about three yards away.

Francis and Nate climbed into the trailer, carrying Mfumbe with them. Kayla scrambled in behind. As she closed the back doors, she saw other prisoners darting out the opening in the Waters Shed. She also witnessed a G-1 officer racing around to the back of it. The prisoners dispersed in various directions, and she didn't have time to find out if any were recaptured.

The truck sped off, lurching forward so strongly that she could barely latch the door before sliding across the back of the trailer.

She had Mfumbe back . . . but what would they do now?

CHAPTER 8

They couldn't bring Mfumbe to a hospital and risk the chance that he'd be taken back into custody. "But we can't keep him in the truck or the garage," Dusa said. "He needs help."

They were back at the Drakians' garage. Mfumbe had been sleeping while Kayla sat beside him and read through his slim volume of poetry to pass the time. When he finally awoke, his right eye could barely open. This was bad, but the blood he started coughing up was even more worrisome to Kayla. "What about going to your parents?" she suggested.

"There's no way," he told her. "My father and I weren't even talking when I left home the last time."

Kayla had been reading a poem called "The Death of the Hired Man" by Robert Frost. "'Home is the place where, when you have to go there, They have to take you in,'" she said, reading a line from the poem.

Mfumbe grunted unhappily. "Easy for him to say," he mumbled, turning onto his side. "He didn't know my father."

By the end of the day, however, they were once

again on the Superlink, this time headed north toward Mfumbe's home. Despite his objections, none of them could come up with an alternate plan to take care of him. His parents were bar-coded. They probably had private doctors they could take him to see. There didn't seem to be any other choice, so Mfumbe had reluctantly consented to go.

On the ride up, Mfumbe sat between Kayla and Dusa and slept most of the way. Kayla told Dusa about seeing Eutonah.

"This psychic stuff is so weird," Dusa commented.

"When I was in the mountains, Eutonah taught me a lot," Kayla replied. "She's amazing at harnessing the power of her mind. She says I was born with natural ability as a psychic, but I need a lot more training."

Mr. and Mrs. Taylor lived in a neat house on a suburban street. Mfumbe's mother burst into tears when he appeared on her doorstep at dawn the next morning, supported by Dusa on one side and Kayla on the other. Overjoyed to see him, she asked no questions as she ushered them into their living room. His father fumed at first, but seeing the condition his son was in, he soon relented and phoned a friend of his whose son was a doctor.

"Kayl-l-a and Dusa can stay here, right?" Mfumbe checked with his parents.

Kayla looked at him sharply. The quiver, the odd stammer on the *l* sound in the way he'd said her name — she'd never heard that in his voice before. He was probably just weak.

The Taylors exchanged an uncomfortable glance at each other. "It could be dangerous," he said.

"You're right," Dusa said firmly. "You might want to consult a lawyer after he sees a doctor."

"But he's bar-coded now," Mrs. Taylor pointed out. "Everything is all right now."

"They grabbed so many people and bar-coded them that they might not even bother to look for him," Dusa allowed. "But we did break him out of jail and —"

"You broke him out of jail?" Mr. Taylor shouted.

Kayla stepped toward Mfumbe's father. "They hurt him and we thought that —"

Mr. Taylor wheeled around so that he was looking Kayla directly in the face. "I don't care what you thought!" he shouted at her. "My son was headed for a university education on a full scholarship until he got mixed up with you! Thanks to you, he's lost that chance. He might be wanted by the police. He has a criminal record for shoplifting."

"He just took a bottle of Adleve, dear," Mrs. Taylor defended Mfumbe.

"Yes, and he stole it for *her*!" Mr. Taylor insisted. "Every mess he's gotten into is because of her." He took a small phone from the pocket of his cardigan sweater. "In fact, the last I recall, the Yorktown police are still looking for this girl in connection with her mother's death. I think it's my duty to call them."

"Dad, no!" Mfumbe shouted. The effort set him into a fit of coughing.

"He's coughing up blood!" Mrs. Taylor realized. While she and her husband attended to Mfumbe, Dusa and Kayla slipped out the door.

Dusa's fake bar code tattoo was made from the records of a woman who had died with an active bank account that still contained close to two hundred dollars. They used it to buy lunch at a diner in Peekskill. As they ate, Kayla asked her about the fake tattoos.

"This computer hacker genius out west does them for us, Jack something or other," Dusa explained. "He takes them from the files of dead people. We like to spread the fakes around, to make them available to people who might need them but don't know where to get them. In fact, I'm heading out to Nevada to get another batch. I have to meet a bunch of people in Yorktown to set it up as soon as we leave here. I can't bring you to the meeting because it's top secret."

An elderly waiter served them thick slabs of the chocolate cake they'd ordered. "I just saw you on the TV," he said to Kayla. He pointed to the fake bar code on her wrist. "You were saying how much you love your bar code."

"That's my sister," Kayla mumbled.

"Do you like your bar code, too?" the waiter asked. Kayla noticed his wrinkled wrist was also coded.

"Not much," she admitted.

"Me, neither," the waiter agreed, "but I can't get in to see the doctor without it, so what could I do?"

"I know. It's tough to do anything if you don't have one," Kayla sympathized politely. So many people were just stuck with it.

After lunch, Kayla and Dusa walked down to the Peekskill GlobalTrak BulleTrain station beside the river. When they got there, Dusa went into the station office to meet her Nevada connection. Before leaving, Kayla couldn't stop herself from glancing up at the window of the apartment across the road where Zekeal Morrelle had once lived.

The ramshackle apartment was at the top of a long, narrow wooden staircase that ran up the side of the building, above Vinnie's Tattoo Parlor. Vinnie's was now boarded up, since all permanent decorative tattoos had been made illegal. She recalled reading that Gene Drake had once worked in Vinnie's as a tattoo artist. That was how he had come to work for Global-1 as a bar code tattoo "provider."

Kayla remembered the apartment, and how she'd been so crazy about Zekeal back then. They'd been together there so many nights, so close — or so she'd thought. She had believed he loved her until the night she discovered he was really a Tattoo Generation agent.

What an emotional wipeout that had been! Total mind-boggling betrayal.

It had been the same night that her mother, in a drugged up, crazed state, had tried to burn her bar code off her wrist, accidentally setting the kitchen curtains ablaze. Gas from the stove had finished the job, igniting the entire house into an inferno.

From that night on, Kayla had been on the run. It was strange now to be here. She stared up at the apartment, remembering the days when she'd loved Zekeal.

And then the door opened and he stepped out onto the outside staircase landing.

CHAPTER 9

Kayla stepped back quickly into the shadowy station doorway. Could he see her there across the road staring up at him? He didn't appear to, though she pressed her aching back more firmly against the door, just to be sure.

He was dressed in a jumpsuit, the official Tattoo Gen uniform. One of his eyes was covered with a black patch. Had she done that? According to the article in *The Lake Placid News,* she and Mfumbe had "brutally attacked" him. In reality, he and the others from Tattoo Gen were the ones who had violently raided their encampment atop Whiteface Mountain. Kayla had been shot and Mfumbe had been trying to protect her when Kayla used her psychic powers to drop a tree limb onto Zekeal. She hadn't intended to blind him, but obviously she had, in one eye.

Oh, well, she thought coldly. She couldn't believe he'd ever meant so much to her. Briefly, she wondered if he was still involved with Nedra Harris. The petite fascist was now the national spokesperson for Tattoo Gen. The two of them deserved each other.

Zekeal went back inside just as a GlobalTrak BulletBus came around the corner. Kayla ran across the street to catch it. Her heart skipped a beat with nervous anticipation as, climbing up to the bus's scanner, she flashed her fake bar code for payment. The scanner beeped her through. It had worked!

The BulletBus traveled silently toward her house, running smoothly on its underground electromagnetic track, passing so many familiar sights. She went by the crummy motel where her best friend, Amber Thorn, had been forced to live after something in her parents' bar codes had derailed their lives. Unable to get a mortgage, her father fired from his job, even denied fuel for their cars, the Thorns had moved to Nevada to live with a relative, an eccentric aunt who nonetheless possessed a viable bar code tattoo.

The last time she'd received an e-mail from Amber was the previous May. Amber's Aunt Emily was against modern advances like computers, but Amber had reached Kayla from an Internet address at a cybercafé in Carson City. Apparently, Aunt Emily was driving the family insane with her strict, weird ways. Amber had sounded pretty miserable.

Kayla's last attempt at communicating with Amber had been in September, on the very day she and Mfumbe had decided to join the Decode March on Washington. It had been her turn to act as runner, and she'd delivered a batch of handwritten letters to one of the Postmen.

The BulletBus continued past Artie's Art Supply, or at least where Artie's Art Supply had once been. Now the store was gone and a HealthBurger concession stood in its place. Kayla remembered how she'd shown up for work one afternoon only to discover that the store was locked and that Artie, his wife, and his two little girls, all of whom had lived above the store, were gone. Artie and his wife were not bar-coded. Kayla wondered what had become of them.

After a few minutes, Kayla got off the BulletBus on a residential street of narrow, attached row houses. Before reaching her own home, she came to the house where Gene Drake had lived with Francis and Nate.

She gasped at the sight of a small terrier sitting on the front steps. Gene's dog! It sat amid bouquets of flowers in front of a door heavily graffitied with various slogans and remarks done by different writers. GENE DRAKE WAS A HERO! GENE DRAKE (1997–2025) HIS SPIRIT LIVES ON. GLOBAL-1 WILL BE UNDONE!!

Some of the bouquets were wilted, even dead, but new ones lay on top. Someone had attempted to rub off the writing, but fresh comments were scrawled over the smear of erasures.

A young boy came around from the back of the house and put a leash on the terrier's collar. "Stop coming here every day!" he scolded the dog, his voice warm with affection despite his sharp words.

"You're our dog now," he added as he tugged the dog away from the steps.

Strange, Kayla thought, not for the first time, that an odd character like Gene Drake — heavyset and badly groomed, reeking of cigarette smoke, nervous and uncharismatic — should be so deified and adored after his death.

A red leaf dropped from a nearby maple tree. Then another fluttered to the ground. A wind was blowing them all down, one by one. She watched them fall, forgetting about everything else. . . .

* * *

She is standing in a desert, a hot breeze burning her skin. Blue mountains in the far distance. Feelings of hatred. Rage. Murderous thoughts. She will show them all the power of her genius, show what a mind expanded many times beyond its usual dimensions can do. If they want to play God, she can play God, too. They will not cage her, no matter what!

* * *

Someone walked up beside her. His presence jolted her back to reality.

"Postal delivery," said the young man in dark glasses standing beside her. A Postman. He handed her an envelope with the name Kayla Marie Reed written on it.

"How did you find me?" she asked him.

"The kid with the terrier saw you," he replied as he walked away.

Kayla glanced down at the handwriting on the envelope. It was a script she knew well.

She smiled.

PART 2

Ye shall know the truth,
and the truth shall make you mad.

Aldous Huxley

CHAPTER 10

Kayla looked out the window as the East/West CrossLink blasted by at top speed. The monotony and sameness of the passing cars, the flat, dusky landscape, and the endless highway lulled her. She leaned her head against the cab's passenger window. Her eyes were wide open, but she was no longer seeing the highway. . . .

* * *

She's moving through a dilapidated tenement, panting as she goes. A rat scrambles by her feet. She stops and opens a pack. It's her own pack. Hastily, she tosses out old clothes, a sketch pad, charcoal pencils, anything that she can't sell. She throws the bag angrily onto the floor. Useless! She checks her sneering image in a chipped hallway mirror. Not Kayla's look, but it's definitely her face beneath the heavy makeup.

* * *

Dusa was speaking to her from the driver's seat

of the truck. Kayla jumped at the sound of her voice.

"What?" Kayla asked.

"I said, I have to stop in St. Louis," Dusa repeated. "A guy there is giving me a chip with a lot of records on dead people. Wow! You were in another world."

"Daydream, I guess." Kayla hadn't yet told Dusa about the visions she sometimes had. This one was so strange. Who were these girls she was seeing? They looked like her — but so different. Alternate selves? Alternate possible futures? It was incredibly unnerving, and she wasn't ready to talk about it.

"Are you okay?" Dusa checked.

"Yeah. Fine," Kayla replied. They'd been driving for two days. Their destination: Carson City, Nevada. The letter she'd received from Amber had sounded desperate.

I can't do this anymore, Kayla. I feel like I'm completely surrounded by insanity at every turn. Aunt Emily is a total nut job. I call her Tarantula Woman because she keeps a tank of them in her bedroom and they're forever escaping.

Dad left for California saying he was going to find a job but I think he just plain split. We haven't heard from him in a month. My brother took off with some bikers shortly after that. Mom's hair is falling out from nerves and all she does is worry about it all day. I have no friends at all. Some days I can't even get the words out but there's no one to talk to so it hardly matters. I miss you. I think I'll just walk off into the desert and keep going until I turn into dry, sandy dirt and blow away.

When Kayla had met up with Dusa again near the tractor trailer hidden in the woods, she'd asked to come along on the trip out west, maybe get a ride to Carson City. From there she'd set out to look for Amber. Her friend needed her — and what use was Kayla's friendship if she didn't show up for her?

"What about Mfumbe?" Dusa had asked.

"I think he's stuck where he is for a while," Kayla had answered with a resigned sigh. Just to be sure, she found a quiet spot on a boulder in the woods and tried to contact him, mind to mind. She received his reply but it was weak and troubled. *Doctors have given me druggy medicine. Feel rotten, always sleepy. Don't come to the house. My father called G-1. Looking for you.*

"It might not be such a bad idea for you to go west for a while," Dusa had said when Kayla told her what she'd learned from Mfumbe. "Eutonah also said G-1 is looking for you. I wonder why."

"Me, too."

"I say we hit the road right now. Why wait?"

She'd been right, Kayla had thought. Why sit around and wait for Global-1 to catch her? She might as well go this very moment.

* * *

They slept in the back of the truck at a campground outside Pittsburgh where they arrived around three that morning. At eight A.M. Kayla awoke in the passenger seat in the cab of the moving truck. "I don't even remember coming up front," she mumbled, rubbing her eyes.

"I woke you up, but I think you were just walking in your sleep," Dusa said with a chuckle. "Go back to sleep if you want."

That sounded like a good idea to Kayla, but she found that sleep wouldn't come. She had never seen much of America other than the northern East Coast. The passing scenery was much the same along the East/West CrossLink; fields and towns and malls followed by more of the same. The billboards that dotted the CrossLink advertised the same radio stations and the same superchains of stores and places to eat. Kayla remembered a poem that Mfumbe had read to her as they walked along the Hudson River on their way to Washington. It was by a nineteenth-century poet named Walt Whitman. *I hear America singing, the varied carols I hear.* The poet wrote about working people busy with their various activities.

Kayla had particularly loved the last lines, and she recalled them easily.

Each singing what belongs to him or her and to none else,

The day what belongs to the day — at night the party of young fellows, robust, friendly,

Singing with open mouths their strong melodious songs.

The poem conjured an image of robust individuals embracing their own unique qualities and together forming a song that was America. When had all this conformity and sameness set in? How had it happened? When had the varied carols turned into a single corporate advertising jingle?

And yet she knew so many strong individuals. People were still people, as varied as ever, if they were only given a chance to be themselves.

In St. Louis late that afternoon, they stopped to eat at a diner overlooking the Mississippi River. Outside the large picture window, the sunset bounced off the river's powerful and choppy brown current. "How much money is left in your fake bar code account?" Kayla asked as she turned away from the river to peruse the many laminated pages of the menu.

"Not sure exactly," Dusa admitted. "It could run out at any time. We might just have to bolt if the code comes up empty."

"Great," Kayla said with a cynical laugh. Would the day ever come when she wouldn't have to be prepared to run at a moment's notice?

Their waitress studied Kayla with particular

interest. “Congratulations,” she said after she’d taken down the order.

“What for?” Kayla asked cautiously.

“You know,” the waitress said, seeming to assume Kayla was joking. “It’s great that you’ve gotten your life sorted out.”

“The ad,” Kayla realized when the waitress had gone. “She thinks I’m the girl in the ad.”

“So do a lot of people,” Dusa pointed out as she got up to go to the ladies’ room. When she returned she carried a newspaper and her face wore an odd expression.

“What?” Kayla asked.

She tossed the paper onto the table. The front pages were folded back revealing the Life & Style section within. Kayla’s eyes widened. The title of the lead story was FORGIVENESS AND ACCEPTANCE BUILD A NEW DREAM. A picture of the clean-scrubbed Kayla who had appeared on TV was under the title — and she wasn’t alone. Beside her was Zekeal. The two of them held hands and stared lovingly at each other.

FORGIVENESS AND ACCEPTANCE BUILD A NEW DREAM

October 17, 2025 — Who says people can't change? Don't tell that to Kayla Marie Reed! She knows that it's not so. The 17-year-old with the sunny smile has a lot to be happy about these days, but she's been through some tough times.

You may have seen her sincere testimony on TV. It concerns the inner journey she's been on, searching her conscience in regard to the bar code tattoo. In the poignant public service announcement, Kayla Marie recounts how, through rehabilitation counseling provided to her by Global-1 Psychiatric Outreach, she overcame a crippling trauma brought on by her presence at the Putnam Valley Tattooing Center the day that Gene Drake opened fire on innocent citizens.

Before this recovery could take place, however, Kayla became embroiled in the anti–bar code resistance headed by the group calling itself Decode. Breaking ties with friends and loved ones, Kayla Marie joined dissident groups hiding in the mountain ranges of northern New York

State. Desperate to find his girlfriend, Tattoo Generation agent Zekeal Morrelle pursued her to the mountains only to be brutally beaten by Kayla Marie and a band of her violent cohorts. The price was high. A blow to Zekeal's head cost him the sight in his right eye.

"I was so deluded," Kayla Marie says now, a bit embarrassed and ashamed. "I actually believed at the time that I had psychic powers. I thought I caused a branch to fall on Zekeal's head by using my mental abilities. How ridiculous!"

"I forgive her," Zekeal is quick to add. "We're engaged to be married now. I know we're young, and we'll wait a few years before we tie the knot, but we want to be engaged."

Kayla Marie, who has a lifelong interest in art, has just been named the youth director of Tattoo Generation's Public Murals Program. She will be in charge of designing and overseeing the painting of murals that depict the convenience and desirability of having a bar code tattoo.

"It is so fulfilling to finally be able to use my art," Kayla Marie says.

CHAPTER 11

The next day, Kayla left Dusa standing by the famous St. Louis arch so she could meet her contact. He'd give Dusa records of people who were dead, to be used in making fake bar codes.

Kayla walked down by the Mississippi, past a row of seaside restaurants. She shifted her pack on her shoulder. In it was an e-chip Dusa had entrusted to her. "It's got info on Drakians all over the county," Dusa had revealed as she'd slipped it into Kayla's bag. "I don't want to be carrying it when I meet this guy, just in case he isn't who he says he is."

Steamships came into the harbor. For a fee they took tourists for rides on the river. This might be a good time to test the fake bar code she wore to discover if it contained a bank account. She got in line, and to her pleased surprise, her fake rang through with the correct amount for her admittance. Her name rang up as Rose Wahmann.

When she got to the entrance gate, the attendant reached for her backpack. "You'll need to check that for security reasons," he said.

Kayla remembered the e-chip. It would make her feel safer if she kept that with her. "Let me just take out my wallet first," she requested, working the buckles of the pack.

She was reaching into the bag when someone shoved her forcefully from behind. The impact came on the same spot where she'd been hit in Washington. It caused a searing pain to run down her back, dropping her to her knees.

"Hey!" the attendant shouted at the figure who dashed past Kayla. "She has your bag!"

Kayla stood up and took off at full speed in pursuit of the fleeing figure. Despite the pain in her back, she knew she couldn't lose the e-chip. Whether this was a straightforward mugging or something more deliberate she didn't know, but she couldn't let that e-chip get to the wrong people.

She grew closer to the running figure as they raced along the riverside walkway. It was a female in a red hooded sweatshirt and the silver stretch jeans that had come into style. The hood was raised, obscuring the thief's face and hair.

The thief raced off the walkway, hopping a chain-link fence. Kayla wasn't sure she could be as agile but spotted a break in the fence several feet farther up. Running through the opening gave her a slight advantage since she was able to close in diagonally on the thief.

She continued to pursue the thief onto a narrow street filled with antique shops and hardware stores. The restored storefronts looked as though they were from early in the past century. The girl ducked into an alley, and Kayla followed her in. A flash of the red hood was all she glimpsed as the thief rounded the corner at the end of the alley. Starting to pant heavily, Kayla kept on her trail.

When she emerged from the alley she saw a hint of red dart into a doorway three buildings up on a quiet block of dilapidated, run-down tenements. Kayla continued up the block to the building.

Sucking in gulps of air, she stared at the building with its boarded-up windows. How brave did she feel? She shook off the question. There was no choice but to get that bag back.

She pulled open the splintered purple front door. Inside, the hall was dark, lit only with the filtered sunlight from a filthy side window beside the peeling door. A hideous smell assaulted her, and she saw that some animal had relieved itself in the corner.

Cautiously, she climbed the steep, narrow stairway. In the halls, doors had been removed from their hinges and apartments were empty. The handle of a broken hammer lay on the floor on the first landing, and she stooped to pick it up for protection. It was heavy and had a jagged, broken end that could prove dangerous to anyone coming at her.

She paused on the second-floor landing, clutching her weapon more tightly. Footsteps echoed from above her. Tilting her head slightly, she listened closely. How many people were up there?

As best as she could tell — just one.

Barely daring to breathe, she crept up the remaining stairs and entered another apartment that had been deprived of its front door. Lines of bright sunlight crept through the cracks in the boarded windows, affording her just enough light to see. She was in what had once been the living room and followed the sound of the footsteps toward a shadowy hall.

The thief stood at the far end of the hall digging through Kayla's pack, impatiently tossing its contents onto the cracked linoleum floor.

Ducking into the empty room nearest her, Kayla peered around the doorway. She'd seen this place before. Where?

As the thief tossed the bag in disgust and pushed back her red hood, Kayla knew exactly where she'd seen it — in her vision!

The girl turned toward a cracked mirror hanging on the wall behind her. As she looked at herself, Kayla saw her, too. Overbleached platinum hair. Heavily made-up eyes and a smear of bloodred lipstick.

And Kayla's face.

Kayla covered her mouth in surprise, but not in time. The girl heard her involuntary gasp of shock and whirled toward it.

Kayla stepped out into the hall, firmly clenching

the broken handle. "You stole my pack," she said, stepping forward. "I need it back."

"Take it," the thief said, belligerently jerking her chin toward the bag. "There's nothing worth crap in it, anyhow."

As Kayla grew closer, the girl could see her more clearly. "Wait a minute," she said, a nervous shake coming into her voice. "I've seen you before, it was . . ."

"In a vision," Kayla finished.

"Yeah," the girl agreed softly, staring at Kayla, her black-rimmed eyes widening with every step Kayla advanced. "In my mind I saw you at the steamboat. I saw you, but only from the back. I thought it meant that you had something in your pack that would be worth a lot. That you'd be a good mark. And sure enough, when I went down there today — there you were."

Kayla asked, "Don't you notice something else? Can't you see how alike we are?"

Apparently, the superficial differences between them were all the girl saw. She cocked her head to the side and gazed at Kayla with complete incomprehension.

Kayla went to the girl's side and faced the mirror. "Look," she urged. The two faces were aligned perfectly beside each other. The girls were the same height, their faces the same shape, their noses had the same slope, their foreheads the same width. If Kayla had wanted to become identical to this other person, all she'd have to do was bleach her hair and pile on makeup. With a quick glance at the girl's wrist, Kayla saw she had no bar code.

The girl got it. The fact was evident in the amazed, slightly unnerved expression on her face. "This is banged out," she murmured.

"What's your name?" Kayla asked.

"Kara."

Kayla turned to her, disbelief written across her face. Could they be twins separated at birth?

"Where were you born?" Kayla asked.

"Somewhere in Missouri."

"You don't know exactly where?"

Kara shook her head. "I don't remember where my first foster home was. I was in a bunch of them until I split from the last one and went solo."

"How long ago was that?" Kayla asked.

"Just before I turned seventeen. I don't know — March, I think. I remember everything was real muddy the day I took off. It was pouring rain."

Kara showed Kayla the large empty room where she slept on a fake fur coat she'd found in a Salvation Army donation bin. She showed her the drawings she'd done of her visions. She had a pile of them that she kept in a musty, cobweb-crossed closet. When she pulled them out, she had to brush rodent droppings from their surfaces. "Damn rats," she muttered without too much agitation. This was how her life was, and she seemed resigned to it.

The pencil drawings were crude, their perspective

awkward in places. Yet Kayla thought they indicated a deep natural ability for art. They were vivid in their detail, and their bold lines seemed expressive of the artist's intense reaction to everything she saw, both the ugly and the beautiful.

"These are unbelievable," Kayla murmured as she inspected them one by one. Even more than the execution of the drawings, it was their subject matter that held her there, fascinated.

The first was a drawing of a house on fire — Kayla's house.

"That was a vision I had last spring, sometime around May. I heard a woman shouting, and then this crazy fireball roared up the hall," Kara recalled with a shiver. "It was different from the vision I've been having since I was thirteen. It's a different house from the one in the other vision."

"Tell me about the other vision," Kayla said.

Kara pulled a drawing from the pile and put it on top. It was a pencil drawing of a house burning. A girl of about seven or eight was standing outside it, laughing as flames engulfed the building. The girl bore a striking resemblance to Kara. It could have been Kayla, too.

"Is this you?" Kayla asked, pointing to the girl in the picture.

"I don't know," Kara admitted. "In the vision I'm never sure. It seems to be me, and yet I don't know any of the people I'm thinking about or recognize the house."

"So much fire," Kayla noted, half to herself.

Kara nodded, taking the drawings and studying them as if for the first time. "I was banged out about it for weeks, afraid it meant this firetrap dump was going to go up in smoke. I still worry about it."

"It isn't *your* future," Kayla told her, speaking quietly. "One drawing is of my house. It burned last May."

"Your house?" Kara asked, stunned.

"Yes, and this other house has a child in it, this laughing child. It's not my house, and it isn't this building."

"I wonder if one of us will have a child who looks like this in the future."

Kayla studied Kara's face, now fixed into an expression of almost childlike awe by the full realization that she was staring at a twin. Without the hard expression she'd worn at first, she looked even more like Kayla. And there was clearly a mental connection between them.

"Do you have any idea who your parents are?" Kayla asked cautiously, uneasy about posing such a sensitive question.

Kara laughed bitterly. "At my last foster home they hinted that she was some kind of addict, but I don't know if that was real or they were just being their evil selves. I had to escape before they made me get that banged-out bar code on my birthday. When you make your life on the street, you don't need one. I see you don't have a real one. You can spot the fakes if you know what to look for. They start to flake a little after a while. The real tattoo doesn't. Why don't you have one? Not seventeen yet?"

"I turned seventeen on April sixteenth," Kayla replied.

Kara's jaw fell. "Me, too! April sixteenth!"

"We *must* be twins!" Kayla said.

Kara held up three fingers.

"You had a vision of another one of us?" Kayla dared ask. "Was it someone in a desert? Someone . . . frightening?"

Kara shook her head. "No, I saw someone reading palms. She was good at it, too, because she was like me."

"What do you mean, like you? Could you see her face?"

"No, it was more like I was thinking her thoughts, looking out of her eyes," Kara revealed. "But she was a good palm reader because she had the same ability as me."

"What ability?" Kayla asked.

"I can see the future. She can, too, but she pretends she sees it in palms. She doesn't. It's the visions. Her visions come faster than mine."

Kayla realized that it meant that there were four of them, three of whom could see visions of the future. Could the girl in the desert see ahead, too? She moved the picture of the child and the burning house to the bottom of the pile and looked at the next drawing, a desert landscape with a blue tent standing in the middle of the vast desert emptiness. "I've had a vision like this, too," she told Kara. "I saw this same scene in one of them, only I didn't see the tent."

"Crazy," Kara murmured. "I should tell you that I'm pretty sure somebody's looking for me."

"Your parents," Kayla guessed.

"No. I don't know who it is, but someone tried to grab me the other night when I came back late. Another time before that, two men chased me. I can't let them get me. I have a feeling they know I have visions."

Kayla recalled her meeting with Eutonah in the Waters Shed jail. She'd warned her that Global-1 was looking for her — and not just because she didn't have a bar code tattoo or even for her supposed involvement in her mother's death in the fire. Why, then? And why were they also searching for this other girl, Kara, who was identical to her?

Suddenly, Kayla's problems seemed much bigger and more complex than they had been before.

CHAPTER 12

"Thank God you didn't lose that e-chip," Dusa said that night when she and Kayla were once again on the East/West CrossLink blasting down the halogen-illuminated superhighway at top speed. "We have to have all that info so we can find one another. If that stuff had gotten into the hands of G-1 . . ." She shuddered, her shoulders quivering. "Turned out my contact was on the level, and I got the records with no problem. But I couldn't chance having that chip on me in case it was a setup."

Kayla nodded, but she was only half listening. She couldn't stop thinking about Kara. She'd left her in that abandoned building, subsisting as a petty thief rather than be bar-coded. There hadn't been any way to take her along — it would have been too risky.

Although the girl was uneducated and rough, Kayla saw herself in Kara. They were both artistic, loved to draw. Both had an instinctive aversion to the bar code tattoo. And they had seen the same vision, gazing through a stranger's eyes out into a desert landscape.

As Dusa and Kayla approached a brightly illuminated billboard on the CrossLink, Dusa let out a low, long whistle. "Would you look at that," she said. "You're all over the place, kiddo!"

Kayla's smiling face appeared splashed across the giant sign, hundreds of feet high. Her hair was perfect. Her teeth gleamed with the unnatural incandescence of the digitally retouched. Above her was written: I LOVE MY BAR CODE TATTOO!

"That makes me want to scream!" Kayla cried. It enraged her that someone was using her image to promote the thing she hated most in the world.

"Scream if you like, but we can do better than that." Dusa eased the truck off the highway and onto the shoulder. Leaning over, she opened the glove compartment and removed what looked like a foot-long aluminum tube. "Wait here," Dusa advised as she slipped out of the truck.

Kayla peered out the window as Dusa moved quickly to the sign and scrambled up the ladder to its bottom platform, disappearing into the darkness behind it. She looked at the image of her face and was struck by a thought that made her draw in a quick breath of stunned surprise.

What if this girl wasn't a digital fake? What if she was another look-alike, the same as Kara? If so, it meant that, at the very least, there were five of them!

Dusa jumped back into the truck, tossed her aluminum bar to the floor, and turned on the engine. "We'd better get going fast," she said, already pulling onto the CrossLink.

"What did you do?" Kayla asked.

"That tube's a welder's torch." A deeply self-satisfied grin slowly spread across Dusa's face. "Look out your side mirror."

Kayla gazed at the billboard's reflection in the side mirror as a line of flame caught hold and raced up its right side. In seconds, the fiery sign was illuminating the black night sky.

They left the CrossLink and turned onto the old Nevada State Highway 487 and went six more miles to the small town of Baker near the Great Basin Desert. "It's the largest desert in the United States," Dusa told Kayla. "The Mojave Desert is to the south of it and so is the Sonoran Desert."

"It sounds like a whole lot of desert," Kayla commented.

"More than three times the size of England," Dusa agreed. "It's surrounded by the Rocky Mountains on the east and the Sierra Nevada Mountains to the west."

"Are we going into the desert?" Kayla asked.

"Yes, we are," Dusa confirmed. "Just hope the air-conditioning holds out."

After purchasing more than twenty gallons of water in Baker, they drove into the desert.

Kayla wondered again about her vision, remembering Kara's drawing and being unnerved by how much it resembled what she was now seeing outside her window. But if it was a vision, why was she thinking those insane, egomaniacal thoughts? It was as troubling a question as wondering why she would ever advocate the bar code tattoo.

Dusa stopped the truck at the wide entrance of a limestone cave. Several young men and women instantly appeared at the cave's mouth to greet them. They were all dressed for high heat. They surrounded Dusa, obviously very pleased by her arrival. Nate and Francis were among them and stepped forward to hug her. She spoke with them animatedly as the group moved back toward the cave's entrance.

The minute Kayla emerged from the truck, the heat overtook her, sending her staggering backward. She had the panicked feeling of not being able to catch her breath. When she put her hand on the truck to steady herself, she was amazed at how the surface burned. She quickly drew her hand back. The undulating heat waves emanating from the desert floor gave her the disconcerting feeling that she was gazing into a body of water as she looked out onto the vast expanse of lowland.

"Oh, yeah. It's hot," said a lean, muscular guy wearing army fatigue shorts, a sleeveless white T-shirt, and an amused smile. A fuzz of blond hair covered his head. "It's crazy hot out here, but it's not so bad in the cave." She thought she detected a hint of an accent. Irish? English? She wasn't sure. He extended his hand to her. "I'll help you inside."

Kayla preferred to walk without help. She

stepped forward, declining his offered hand. She instantly hit another wall of heat.

"You'll get used to it," the young man assured her, taking her hand. This time Kayla let him steady her.

As she walked with him toward the cave, she couldn't help noticing that he was very attractive.

CHAPTER 13

"When we used to have a national parks program they would give tours through these caves," Dusa told her that same evening as they wiped the plates from dinner clean with dry cloths; those charged with washing them with water wanted to use as little of it as possible. "Now these caves are all ours. The Adirondacks were becoming too well known as resistance central. After last summer's raids we knew it wasn't safe up there anymore. A bunch of Drakians discovered that these caves were unused and made this our new headquarters about three months ago."

Kayla remembered the news article Nedra Harris had written suggesting that the Drakians had relocated away from the Adirondack Mountains. Kayla wondered if all the groups were dispersing across the country. It might be a good thing to spread the resistance rather than have it all in one spot.

"Take a look around," Dusa went on. "The stalactites and stalagmites are pretty amazing. I'd show you myself, but right now I have to go over these files with Jack that I brought in."

"Jack?" Kayla asked.

Dusa nodded at the guy who had helped Kayla into the cave. He stood talking seriously with Nate and Francis just inside the entrance. All through dinner Kayla had tried to refrain from stealing glances at him, but she found it difficult. Aside from his good looks, there was something she found compelling in the athletic, confident way he carried himself.

"He's the technology genius who converts these dead-person files into fake bar codes for us. He's so good with computer algorithms that he didn't even bother with college. He was writing incredibly advanced computer code from the time he was eleven. College wouldn't have taught him anything."

"Where's he from?" Kayla asked.

"Belfast, I think."

"He's not exactly a computer geek," Kayla commented with an appreciative grin.

Dusa laughed. "No. Not at all."

Dusa went to talk to Jack, and Kayla walked into the cave, enjoying the increasing coolness. She passed rows of sleeping bags, camping lanterns, and coolers on the rock floor. At one spot, ten computer-chip storage boxes were lined up side by side. She wandered deeper into the cave. Squeezing through a narrow rock pass, she came to a high, wide cavern. Columns of stone formed as towering stalagmites jutting from the cavern floor met massive stalactites dropping from its ceiling.

The space was silent, cool, and incredible. Mfumbe would have been fascinated by it. Kayla wished he was there to see it.

It was funny how often she'd wanted to share something with him. *Look at that mountain. Isn't that sunset incredible?* Nothing seemed as good, or even entirely real, because he wasn't there to share it with her.

What was Mfumbe doing now? Was he still at his parents' home? Was he getting better? In the cool stillness, she closed her eyes and attempted to focus her mind on contacting him. It wasn't words that she hoped to project — at least not at first — but her image and her concern.

She made her mind a blank by focusing on nothing but the sound of her breathing. Slowly in. Even more slowly out.

Breathe in.

Breathe out.

Over and over — until she felt the field of her own energy lift above her body. The walls of the cave no longer contained her, just as her own body could not hold her any longer. She was out on the psychic plane, calling for Mfumbe to contact her.

Then, abruptly, she was back in the cave — back in her body, more aware than ever of its limitations, of pain in her limbs, in her bones, in her skull.

An agonizing burn under her ribs made her clench her fist and ram it into her left side. A debilitating weakness forced her to sit.

Was this what Mfumbe was feeling?

Had she in fact contacted him and taken on his suffering?

An image came to her, spreading behind her clenched-shut eyes. He was in his bedroom, tossing among tangled sheets and blankets. His forehead glistened with sweat, and his eyes were dull in a kind of waking trance. She sensed that he was making a tremendous effort to get out of bed, but something was keeping him from doing it.

Kayla. Too many drugs. Can't think. Where are you? Need to think.

It was as if she could feel the hot slickness of his sweat-soaked skin. She felt the hoarseness in his throat, as though some constriction was stopping him from speaking — and was also now stopping her from breathing.

Don't call or contact in any way. More words came to her, delivered haltingly and with great effort. *Someone is watching here; they're watching for you. Not safe.*

There was so much she wanted to talk to him about. Maybe she counted on him too much, but he was smart and she trusted his judgment. Who did he think Kara might be? What of their shared visions? Why was someone looking for her? Was it as Kara thought, because they could see the future? What did he think she should do next?

All this had to go unsaid and unasked. He was too weak to handle it and she was, too. She didn't know how much longer she could stand this.

I'm still with Dusa. I'm okay. You're hurting, she struggled to tell him. She attempted to project her location to him, thinking of the desert she'd seen so that he might see it.

"Are you all right?" another voice asked.

Startled, Kayla whirled toward the voice, her connection to Mfumbe abruptly snapped.

Gasping great mouthfuls of air, she stumbled back against the cave wall.

Jack had come up behind her noiselessly — or maybe she'd just been too involved with Mfumbe to notice.

"You were somewhere else," Jack said, having observed her trance state. "Someplace pretty banged out. Where'd you go?"

The open, genuine concern in his expression made her want to respond the same way. As the hammering of her heart slowed and the pain subsided, she felt strong enough once again. He sat beside her, listening intently as she told him about how she had learned to communicate telepathically with Mfumbe and others who had gone into hiding in the Adirondacks. She explained how she'd studied with Eutonah, learning to use her mind at a heightened level. "Does it sound too unbelievable to you?" she asked, afraid he might think she was strange or even making it up.

"Why should it? It's like ants," Jack replied.

"Ants?" she questioned.

"Or bees with a hive mind," he went on. "It's called hive mentality when an individual is part of a collective consciousness. It's just another kind of communication, if you think about it. Lots of insects communicate with chemical signals. Ants leave chemical trails that are a kind of collective map. Speech is really a very superficial, limited form of communication. A direct mental link — a psychic connection — gives insight into the mental imagery of the sender."

"I don't know. Is it the same thing? I'm not sure," Kayla admitted. "My teacher, Eutonah, always said that we could tap into a deeper consciousness that was all around us. We did a lot of work with her on it."

"Are there a lot of you psychics now?" he questioned.

Kayla nodded. "Hundreds, I'd guess. Didn't you meet them when you were in the Adirondacks?"

"I was never there. I came on board when the movement started coming west. The Drakians who were in the mountains mostly kept to themselves. They kind of shunned everyone else as being too passive."

"A lot of us were working on our mental powers. I don't think that's passive," Kayla countered, feeling irritation at the criticism.

He began to pace, as if seized with a sudden idea that was making him restless. "No, it's not. It might even be the key."

"The key to what?"

"Gene Drake was onto something, and we've got to find out what it is." His vivid blue eyes brightened with an intense gleam as he warmed to the subject.

"Something worse than our genetics being encoded in the tattoo?" Kayla asked, as though that weren't bad enough.

"Yes, *worse*!" he answered. "And it was in that computer that he gained access to, but he was shot before he could tell anyone."

"He never told Nate or Francis?"

"They say no," he replied. "And the guy who gave him the passwords killed himself the same night Gene was shot."

"How do you know who he was?"

"Nate knew him slightly. He was a brainy computer professor from Caltech. Maybe he was stressed out about Gene or afraid Gene would turn him in."

"Maybe it wasn't really suicide," Kayla suggested.

"That's possible," Jack agreed. "But whatever the reason he killed himself, he's the only person we know of who was able to hack into the Global-1 bar code file."

"Dusa told me *you're* a genius hacker. No luck?"

"I get way into the system, and time after time I hit a block. I've configured and reconfigured the computer algorithms every way I can think of and — no go."

"How could psychics help?" Kayla asked.

"Somebody has to know how to get into that file," he said. "Somewhere on earth, someone has access to that information. Someone who can read minds might be able to discover it."

"We don't exactly read minds," she said.

"Okay, no offense, but you somehow link up mentally, right?"

"Right. But a psychic would have to know who to link up with," she explained. "Any idea who would know the formula?"

"None," he said dismally.

"Maybe somehow we'll find out who it is. Then my psychic strengths or someone else's will be useful. It's stellar to think that all the work we've done on our psychic abilities might really put these G-1 creeps out of business. Then you'd appreciate how important mind strengthening is."

"We work on strengthening the mind here, too. It's very important to us," Jack said. "This is a major struggle we're involved in. We have to be unafraid — physically and mentally strong for it."

Kayla's curiosity was piqued. "How do you work on it? Telepathy?"

"Come on outside and you'll see." He put his hand on her shoulder, guiding her back through the narrow opening.

The cave was empty but she heard voices coming from the front. Something orange-red was aglow on the desert floor. She turned to him, questions in her eyes.

"Are you ready for your first fire walk?" he asked.

CHAPTER 14

Nate went first. The roughly six-foot rectangular bed of glowing coals threw shadows on his face. Drawing in a concentrated breath, he calmed himself, and in the next second he was off, briskly walking barefoot across the coals.

Francis stood in front of the coal bed next. The glow drenched his white undershirt with a vivid, flickering orange.

Images of fire blasted into Kayla's thoughts, seeming to collide with one another. She saw again that searing fireball racing up the hallway of her house. The dream image of her mother, hair ablaze, returned to her with shocking force. She saw her own face alight with flame on the billboard in the night.

Francis took off his wire-rim glasses, drew in a very long breath, and stepped out onto the coals.

Feeling too shaken to watch, Kayla turned away from the group and walked into the desert on her own. A slight breeze carried the pleasant smell of a plant she couldn't identify. The sky was a vast blanket of brilliant stars. In the dark she couldn't see the distant mountains, which made the desert floor seem to stretch on to infinity. She was aware of the low, encouraging murmurs of Drakians behind her, but the farther she walked, the more deeply she was engulfed by the immense silence surrounding her.

Ahead in the distance she spied a flickering spark of light. Curious, she walked toward it. When she had advanced several more yards, she thought she saw a dark figure sitting in front of the light, which she now could smell. A fire.

Something was burning in the fire. It reminded her of the plant smell she'd noticed earlier. As she closed in on the person, she heard a low, rhythmic chanting.

She knew the voice.

"Eutonah?" she spoke into the darkness.

The woman sat in front of the fire, looking very much as she had the first time Kayla had encountered her. She wore a cowboy hat that boasted a wide band of gorgeous feathers. Her tank top and jeans were faded and plain. "The sagebrush makes a nice smoke out here in the desert," she observed calmly, lifting her eyes to watch the rising white smoke.

Kayla crouched near the fire, gazing at her mentor's regal face and fathomless black eyes. "They released you?" she asked.

"They don't have to release what is already free," Eutonah replied.

"You're still in the Global-1 prison?"

"Part of me is, but my spirit can travel, as you know."

"Eutonah, who is looking for me, and why?"

"I have no new information, but I've come to tell you that I have had a strong dream of you. I saw you as a tree with many parts. Lightning struck, and the parts splintered into scattered branches. All the branches came alive and began screaming to be reunited. You are a being that is calling to itself, longing for itself. You must do things you will find terrifying. You must prepare for this by conquering your fears."

"Kayla!" The voice carried through the still night, and she turned toward it. Someone from the group was calling to her. When she turned back to Eutonah, the wise woman was gone. Only her small campfire remained. The scent of sagebrush lingered.

"Kayla!" Someone was walking toward her, calling her name. As the figure grew closer, she recognized the voice as Jack's. She met him halfway. "Why don't you try the fire walk?" he urged when they faced each other. "There's nothing left to be afraid of once you conquer your fear of walking on fire."

Eutonah had dreamed of her as a tree struck by lightning. More fire. She'd instructed her to conquer what she feared most. There were many things she feared. Was fire the greatest?

* * *

Wild terror arose inside Kayla. The desire to run away was close to overwhelming. A fierce heat emanated from the glowing coals, giving her the sensation that her bare feet and ankles were already burning.

She remembered the dream in which she'd gone up in flames. The crowd of Drakians eagerly watched her in silence, no one encouraging her to go forward onto the coals until she was ready. The only advice she'd been given was that once she started she mustn't allow herself to become paralyzed with panic or even to hesitate. "Just keep going, no matter what," Nate had told her.

Like jumping off a high place, she stepped out into the unknown. Her mind was a blank as she moved quickly across the coals.

The soles of her feet were immediately hot, but she wasn't aware of pain. Her only reality was the need to move.

Move!

Move!

Movement became all she was. There was no other Kayla other than Kayla in motion.

And then it was over.

Leaping from the burning coals, she stumbled to her knees and began to sob uncontrollably. If anyone came forward to speak to her, she wasn't aware of it. She buried her face in her hands as wave after wave of powerful emotion threatened to swamp her, to engulf her into their depths.

It was everything. Everything.

Her father's suicide. Her mother, burned to death. Mfumbe gone. Betrayal everywhere. Confusion! The world! How had the world turned into *this* world? How could she live in such a world as this?

She lay on the dry, sandy dirt and drew her knees into a fetal position. Closing her eyes, she fell instantly asleep. And she dreamed.

She dreamed she was on a raft, swirling in a tempestuous storm of raging waves and howling winds. A wave lifted her on its cresting edge only to fling her with reckless abandon into the valley of the next swell. As she clung desperately to the side of the wooden raft, the immense force of the ocean roared around her on all sides.

The raft tilted abruptly just as a jet of flame sprang up at its center. The fire spread in a line, burning upward as the raft was sucked down into a whirlpool, spiraling with increasing speed into the center of the raging sea.

The first heat of the morning desert awoke Kayla. Coming slowly to consciousness, she realized that she was still outside the cave, lying on the desert dirt. She had the sense that she had washed up on some distant shore within herself — a place inside where nothing was any longer as it had been.

CHAPTER 15

When Kayla asked Dusa to take her out to search for Amber, the Drakian was reluctant to leave the task of producing the fake tattoos. But Jack volunteered eagerly. "We can try the swing-lo."

Kayla looked at him, not understanding. "The swing-lo?"

He smiled enthusiastically. "Come on. I'll show you." She followed him out of the cave and along a craggy rock formation at its side. Behind the outcropping was a rickety wooden hut. Its door creaked when he pulled it open.

"Oh, God!" Kayla said, gasping when she saw the patched, round metal machine inside. It had no more than a ten-foot circumference. At its center was a cramped seat well where two people could fit side by side. In front was a computer panel — sleek, high tech, and completely out of keeping with the scrapped-together quality of the rest of the craft. "You built this?" Kayla asked.

He beamed with pleasure. "Sure did! It's an individualized airborne transport. It's the next big thing."

"Where did you get the materials?"

"Everybody here knows about it — they bring

me stuff when they come into the desert. Like Dusa — she brought me this final-level welder's torch so I can smooth out some of the rough edges."

Kayla recalled the flaming billboard. "I saw it," she said. "It's powerful. What makes this go?"

"It runs on magnetic repulsion, but I've done something I don't think anyone has done yet with a vehicle this size. I've amplified the force so that this baby can really fly."

"Like George Jetson?" she asked, recalling the old cartoons from her grandfather's childhood that he had sometimes played for her.

"Yeah, like that," he agreed, "only I don't have the glass dome over the driver's seat, though I suppose it would be easy enough to add. These individual crafts are going to be huge. Everyone's working on a version of one, but I don't think anyone's been able to make them fly like this one can. At least in theory, she should be able to."

"But you haven't tested it yet?"

Jack shook his head. "Not with any weight in it."

"Why do you call it a swing-lo?"

He grinned, seemingly pleased that she'd asked. "Because I'm nuts about that old gospel song you Americans have." He began belting it out in a melodic, pleasant, strong voice.

"I looked over Jordan and what did I see,
Comin' for to carry me home!
A band of angels comin' after me,

Comin' for to carry me home!
Swing low, sweet chariot,
Comin' for to carry me home!
Swing low, sweet chariot,
Comin' for to carry me home!"

His comically sincere rendition of the song was meant to be funny, and it made her laugh. "So this is your sweet chariot?"

"Exactly," he said, grinning even wider, like a proud parent.

"Let's go, then," she suggested. "It's time for a test drive."

He began kicking the wall of the shed, and for a split second Kayla was startled. She even wondered if she'd upset him somehow. Then she realized it was the only way he could get the craft out of the shed, and she instantly joined in, pounding on the wooden wall with sharp kicks.

With their arms shielding their faces, they flinched as the wall gave way and slammed down on the dry, sandy dirt with a resounding bang, sending up a cloud of dust and pebbles. Freed from its wooden casing, the craft gleamed in the desert sun. "Climb in," Jack said, handing Kayla a motorcycle helmet.

Thrilled at the prospect of this wild adventure, Kayla put on the helmet and slid in. Jack sat beside her, his fingers flying as he pressed a series of buttons and toggles.

After a brief, initial hesitation, the craft lifted up with a gentle whirring sound. He hit a button and it lunged forward — but then abruptly stopped, throwing them against the computer. Taking a slim, palm-size computer from his back pocket, Jack fed an adjustment into the swing-lo's circuitry, and the craft lifted once again.

In the next few moments, the swing-lo accelerated to a speed of eighty miles an hour. Kayla knew this from the speedometer readout. Otherwise, without passing trees, houses, or other landmarks, she wouldn't have guessed they were moving that quickly.

Without street regulations or grids to follow, and going at speeds as fast as a hundred miles an hour, Jack quickly brought them to an area of the desert outside Carson City. Hovering there, he typed the name Emily Thorn into his small computer. An address instantly appeared. "Second star to the right and straight on 'til morning," he pretended to read.

"Okay, Peter Pan, what does it really say?" Kayla pressed.

Looking up from the handheld, he pointed at a trailer off in the distance. "If that's trailer twelve, Great Basin Desert, maybe that's it."

They whirred forward, stopping in front of the dented trailer with duct-tape-patched cracked windows. The door flew open and a skinny woman in a shapeless shift faced them, a wide, crude, metal gun in her hand. "Get lost, alien scum!" she shrieked, cocking the gun.

Kayla lifted in her seat to address the woman. "We're not aliens, we —"

The woman fired. Kayla and Jack ducked low as a ball of paint bounced off the side of the swing-lo, spraying them with a fine mist of orange. "It's one of those old paintball guns from back in the last century," Jack realized, laughter in his voice.

"Well, the swing-lo needed a paint job," Kayla pointed out as she bent forward, hands over her head.

Jack peeked up and was instantly hit with a splat of red paint before he could bend back down. "Yes," he said, "and there's more good news. I saw the name on the mailbox. It seems we've found dear Aunt Emily."

Jack jumped out of the swing-lo and ran a zigzag path, dodging Aunt Emily's paintball onslaughts. This maneuver gave her a good enough look at him to be convinced that he was not from another planet. When Kayla followed and asked about Amber, Emily Thorn's face twisted into a snarl of disgust. "A pack of ingrates! The whole family! The bar code knew they were no good. That's why it turned on them, made their lives a living purgatory! The will of the greater good is being served through the bar code."

No wonder Amber had felt she had to escape this woman! "Is Amber here?" Kayla pressed.

"Walked off! Just like the rest of them did. My no-good brother was the first to go. Then his rotten boy took off with some biker gang. The mother is in Carson City Hospital. She got a bad case of TMP."

Jack looked to Kayla. "TMP?"

"Tattoo Mania Psychosis," she explained quickly and quietly. "People get so desperate to get rid of their bar codes that they burn them off. My friend August did it, but sometimes people burn to death or set themselves on fire accidentally. It's how my mother died. Global-1 is trying to tell people it's a form of mental illness."

"What are you two plotting?!" Emily Thorn shrieked. "Speak up so I can hear you!"

"I was explaining about TMP," Kayla said apologetically.

"TMP is a terrible form of insanity," Aunt Emily said, walking toward them. "Losing your mind is a curse on the sinful."

Jack turned his face away from the ranting woman and rolled his eyes at Kayla. She responded with a quick grimace.

Kayla remembered Amber's words from her letter: *I think I'll walk off into the desert and keep going until I turn into dry, sandy dirt and blow away.* She was becoming more and more worried that Amber had done exactly that. Kayla's brief experience of the desert had already taught her that this might be a very short walk. "Do you know where Amber went?" she asked Amber's hostile aunt.

Emily Thorn pointed out into the vastness of the desert. "She just started walking that way."

"Where would she be heading?"

"How should I know?" the woman snapped. "Maybe you *are* alien life-forms, after all. I bet you snuck out of Area fifty-one and you're here to suck my mind dry so you can get the information you need to make us all your slaves."

"That's not it at all," Jack told her. "We only want to find out what happened to your niece."

"Wait here," Emily Thorn barked at him, turning to go into her trailer.

Jack smiled at Kayla, proud of the way he'd smoothed the situation, diverting Emily Thorn with his charm. Kayla wondered how often he used his good looks and engaging smile to get what he wanted.

Emily Thorn emerged from the trailer staggering under the weight of a heavy glass tank. Something was moving inside it. Kayla blinked into the sunlight reflecting off it, not understanding.

Then she remembered Amber's name for Aunt Emily — Tarantula Woman.

"Get 'em, girls!" Emily Thorn shrieked as she

jerked the tank, flinging its contents toward them with surprising strength. Twelve very large tarantulas twitched their furry legs.

"Time to get back in the swing-lo," Jack said quickly, grabbing her by her arm.

Kayla and Jack spent the rest of the morning and the afternoon searching the desert, hovering just above the desert floor in the paint-spattered swing-lo. They saw nothing but sagebrush tumbling aimlessly along. From time to time Kayla was again struck with the sensation that she was looking out on the ocean. When she reported it to Jack, he nodded.

"Everybody sees that out here," he told her. "I guess it's just the heat coming off the land. But, you know, all this was once ocean floor."

It was amazing to her how much the world could change over time. Was it changing even now? Scientists said the temperature had climbed an average of twenty degrees in the past century. The ocean water was turning acidic, the coral was almost all gone. Would the ocean someday be desert, just as this desert had once been ocean?

"I like to think of the water mirage you're talking about as the ghost of the ocean that was once here," Jack said, looking off into the distance.

"A vision of the past rather than of the future," she remarked. "And maybe it's something everyone sees because we all share the same past — at least as a species. Mfumbe says all people have the sight. Some just aren't able to use it yet."

"Makes sense to me," Jack agreed.

"My friend Allyson won a scholarship to study advanced genetics at Harvard. She says genes are everything. She believes that genetic technology is the biggest thing in our future."

"It's sure one of the biggest things. Look how it's changed our world. Your genes affect whether you make it in this world no matter what you do or who you are. As long as we're forced to wear the damn bar code we're all controlled by the genes we were given at birth. Does she like Harvard?"

"She wound up going to Caltech to study nanotechnology instead," Kayla told him.

"Microscopic robots! Final level!" Jack said, pounding the dash of the swing-lo excitedly. "Ever read *There's Room at the Bottom*? It was written in 1959. This complete genius, Nobel Prize–winning guy, Richard Feynman, wrote it, talking about how machinery could be made really, really, really tiny — molecule-size. In 1959! Can you imagine?!"

"Feynman!" Kayla cried, recalling the name from Allyson's letter, the one the Postman had delivered to August. "She's doing research with a professor who studied with Feynman."

Jack threw his hands up in a gesture of longing. "I would do *anything* for a chance like that!" The swing-lo veered sharply to the left before he grabbed the control stick again. "What a great thing for her."

"She had to get a bar code tattoo in order to do it."

He grimaced, his eyes narrowing thoughtfully. "Maybe not; maybe there are some things I *wouldn't* do."

Hunger and the heat compelled them to turn back toward the cave. Jack promised to take her out again the next day to continue the search. When they arrived at the mouth of the cave, Dusa and Francis were outside. "How high did it go?" Francis asked as they hovered and then landed.

"We stayed only five feet above the ground," Jack reported as he hopped out. "I didn't want to push it the first time 'round. It drives smooth and gets great velocity. You can't beat it for going around the desert."

Nate came out and showed them a handheld computer. The screen carried the headlines of an online newspaper. "Read page four when you get a chance," he said. "Some real bad news about David Young."

"What?" Jack asked, concerned. In seconds he brought up the page. Kayla peered over his shoulder, interested in the story. Before she could see it, though, Dusa stepped up to Kayla and put a hand on her shoulder. "I want to show you something," she said, heading for the cave and gesturing for Kayla to follow.

She led Kayla to a low table where a file of freshly minted fake bar code tattoos sat in a pile next to a handheld computer. "Yesterday Jack translated the information in these files into bar codes for us," she said. "He deleted the death dates and any damaging information like health liabilities or criminal records. Today we've been printing them out and making them into fake press-ons."

Kayla's mind was still on the Decode leader, David Young. "Do you know what bad news Nate was talking about?" she asked.

"No. I haven't talked to anyone all day because I've been busy with the fake bar code background checks. And listen." Dusa paused and her eyes shifted uneasily as though she wasn't a hundred percent sure she wanted to proceed. Then she set her jaw and decided to go on. "I think you should see what I found."

Kayla leaned closer, suddenly uneasy. "What is it?"

Dusa held up a hand-size metal box with an infrared glow on one side — a scanner. "I've been scanning new bar codes to make sure they work and to record the info in them. We keep a log of all the deceased people who've contributed to the operation just in case somebody needs to know. While I was scanning, I found something you might be interested in." She took a fake tattoo from her jeans pocket and scanned it. A name came up on the slim computer monitor lying flat on the table: KATHRYN MARIE REED. BORN JULY 6, 1959.

Kayla stared at the words. "Grandma Cathy?" she wondered.

"The file gave a Los Angeles address and other pertinent information, like a social security number, an insurance provider, a California driver's license identification number, and the numbers for a bank account containing twenty-six dollars."

"But my grandmother was Cathy with a *C*," Kayla pointed out.

"Did you ever see it on an official document?" Dusa questioned.

Now that Kayla thought of it, she hadn't. The only time she'd seen it was in her mother's hand, in photo albums that her mother had labeled with the name Grandma Cathy. It was possible that her mother had gotten it wrong. She was dead before Kayla was born, and Kayla's father had spoken of her infrequently. But she *had* lived in Los Angeles and had supposedly died in the psychiatric center she'd been confined to when her schizophrenia became unmanageable.

"There's no genetic code in this file," Kayla pointed out.

"She died in 2015. There's no existing blood sample for her . . . but they could get a health history from her medical records. Drakians have one genetic history that we put into all the fakes. It swears you're the picture of perfect health."

"She was my father's mother," Kayla said. "I never knew either of my grandmothers, but everyone said I looked exactly like Grandma Cathy. We had some pictures of her when she was young. She was holding my father in them, but they were too blurry to really tell what she looked like."

Dusa clicked down the screen, passing more numbers and addresses. "What do you make of this?"

There was a section for listing children. The first one said: JOSEPH REED. BORN NOVEMBER 15, 1979.

"That's my father," Kayla confirmed. "He was an only child."

"Apparently not." Dusa moved farther down the screen. "On April 16, 2008 —"

"That's my birthday!" Kayla said with a gasp.

Dusa nodded. "When she would have been forty-nine years old, Kathryn Marie Reed gave birth to another child, someone named KM-1-6."

As Kayla was absorbing this strange information, Nate and Jack came in, looking somber. "You'd better read this news story about David Young," Nate told Dusa, giving her the handheld scanner.

"Before you do that, Dusa," Jack jumped in, "are we expecting anyone new to come?"

"No. Why?" Dusa replied.

"There's someone on a motorcycle crossing the desert and heading right for the entrance of the cave."

Kayla walked with the others to the front of the cave to see who was approaching. The indistinct moving blur on the wavering desert horizon soon became a clearly visible figure. The driver stopped in front of the cave, and they saw that he carried a satchel bursting with paper.

"Postman," he announced as he approached them with purposeful strides.

"How did you find us?" Dusa demanded, with just a touch of worry in her voice. The Postmen were on their side, but their uncanny ability to track could be unnerving.

"You bought water in Baker," he replied, and there seemed no need for further explanation.

He called out several names of people in the caves, and each eagerly approached him for their letters. "Is Kayla Reed here?" he asked when he had only one letter left in his hand.

"That's me!" Kayla cried, hurrying to him. This had to be from Mfumbe. Maybe he was well enough to travel. She hoped he'd sent her a suggestion for a meeting place.

Then she looked at the envelope and knew immediately it was not his handwriting.

Who else would be trying to contact her?

October 16, 2025

Dear Kayla,

I hope you are well and that this letter finds you. Sorry for not keeping in touch. It's been difficult to reach you for reasons you know better than anyone.

I am writing you now with sad news. August is dead.

It seems unbelievable that someone so full of life would kill himself, but I'm afraid that's exactly what he did. I'm writing because I was sure that you and Mfumbe would want to know. He told me he had become very close to you during the time the three of you spent together.

He and I often wrote, and he kept me up to date on what you were doing. My last letter from him was not like him at all. It was right after he had come back from the march in Washington. It was full of intense sadness. He was down on himself for having given in and gotten the bar code. If I'd been there I'd have reminded him that he had the courage to burn it off, but I'm so far away here in California. Kayla, was there something wrong that he didn't tell me? I know that whole business about trying to contact aliens through telepathy was kind of nuts, but it was hopeful. Augie was always hopeful. That was one of the things I loved about him. I guess there's not much else to say. If you're ever in Pasadena, come by. Just ask anyone how to get to Caltech. Look up Dr. Gold's office in the science department and you'll find me in the research area. I'm almost always there.

I hope you and Mfumbe are well. I admire your courage in continuing to fight this insidious threat to our freedom and dignity as people. It can't be easy. In my research I'm discovering that things are going on that you wouldn't believe. Nanotechnology has had many biological applications since the beginning of the century, but the stuff going on now has the potential to be even more threatening to our freedoms than the bar code tattoo. Better not say any more than that, even in a letter. Come if you can. I'd love to talk to you in person.

Allyson

PS: There are billboards on the freeways out here that show a girl who looks just like you loving the bar code tattoo. I have faith that it's just a digital mock designed to be a mind freak for all the people who've read about you. I'd give money that Nedra is behind it. Those of us who know you don't believe it.

DECODE LEADER ON SUICIDE WATCH IN DC PRISON

Washington D.C. October 19, 2025 — In a shocking new development, former U.S. Senator David Young has been placed on suicide watch, according to prison authorities. Senator Young remains in his DC Global-1 prison cell, refusing to leave despite the fact that his bail of one million dollars has been raised. Senator Young's many supporters in the organization known as Decode, which he founded last year to work for reverses in bar code tattoo legislation, have donated nearly the required amount. Senator Young's father, retired Senator Ambrose Young, former head of the Domestic Affairs Committee, had promised to provide any remaining funds required for his son to make bail.

Senator David Young has vowed to stay in jail until every protester taken into custody during the mass protest of the bar code tattoo in Washington earlier this month is released. These quickly constructed prisons (which have come to be called Waters Sheds after President Loudon

Waters) currently hold 300 remaining protesters whose bar code tattoos reveal information thought to make them a threat to national security.

Late last night, prison doctors said Senator Young became despondent, refusing to eat or drink anything. Guards intercepted a letter he was penning to his Decode followers urging them to give up the fight against the bar code tattoo since it was hopeless.

"He may simply have begun facing reality," says Global-1 warden Garth Webb Rush. "Global-1 provides the bar code as a service to American citizens to facilitate and help organize their daily lives. To contend that there's anything sinister about the bar code tattoo is pure paranoia. I say Senator Young has finally come to his senses."

A source inside the prison told this reporter that Senator Young's despondent state came on him suddenly: "One minute he was energized for the struggle, the next, he was ready to give up. It was like someone threw a switch inside his head and all the fight went out of him. He quickly fell into a slump."

Ambrose Young, who has been staying

at an undisclosed hotel near the prison, feels that the fact that his son was forcibly bar-coded against his will the night of the arrests is at the heart of this depression: "Seven hundred people were bar-coded by force on the night of the arrests. That is a violation that would depress anyone."

Medical staff members treated Senator Young for a persistent hoarseness in his throat before deciding that the condition was an imagined one. "He was very agitated, claiming that his voice was not working correctly," reported a Global-1 doctor. "It was clear to me that he had become delusional when he implied that receiving the bar code tattoo had somehow impaired his ability to speak. Of course, I suppose he could have been speaking metaphorically, but I didn't get that impression. He seemed to feel he was suffering from an actual medical condition brought on by the bar code tattoo."

Global-1, working in close conjunction with the administration of its former chief of operations, President Loudon Waters, defended its actions, arguing that the bar code is law. "If a person doesn't pay his or her taxes, you make that person comply," said President Waters. "If a person does not get the bar code tattoo as dictated by the law of the land, that person must be made to comply with the law." President Waters said this at the airport as he embarked in his private jet for his vacation home on Grand Cayman Island.

CHAPTER 16

Kayla sat beside Jack the next day as they blasted across the desert. "We're heading back in the direction the old crackpot pointed to," he told her. "I've spotted some tire tracks. I don't know — it's something to follow, anyway."

"Okay." Kayla's mind was far away, trying to sort out all she'd learned.

August, dead? Like Allyson, she couldn't believe it.

Guilt gnawed at her like a hungry animal. He had been such a close friend to them in the mountains. She should have searched for him after the Global-1 attack in Washington. She'd simply assumed that because he'd been seen leaving the city he was all right. But he might not have been. And where did he have to go to? The trip back to the Adirondacks would have been difficult, especially if he'd been injured.

"Dusa told me about your friend," Jack said as he drove. "I was sorry to hear it."

"Thanks. This bar code tattoo has brought so much suicide and death with it."

He nodded. "And now David Young is in the pits. Drakians consider his methods a little passive, but we admire him. He's a stand-up guy. I'd hate to see him cave."

"Or worse," Kayla added.

"Yeah, or worse," he agreed somberly.

She'd cried after she received Allyson's letter. Dusa had been comforting, staying with her until she fell asleep from exhaustion and grief.

She'd dreamed of her parents who had died because of the bar code. Amber's mother, who was now near death in a hospital because of it, was also in the dream. Gene Drake joined them, his bullet wounds still oozing blood. He was walking with August. It wasn't a clear dream but hazy, full of ghostly figures who all murmured unintelligibly at the same time, making a maddening babble in her ear.

She'd awakened full of anxiety, remembering what Dusa had told her about the birth of KM-1-6. Had her mother not actually been her real mother?

Was her father really an older brother?

Had her original name been a code that sounded more like a designation of some kind — KM-1-6?

Fear had threatened to paralyze her until she recalled her fire walk. If she could conquer that terror, she could walk through anything. Steeled by the memory, she had gotten up, determined to find Amber. She wasn't going to let another tragedy occur because she hadn't taken the time to search.

A large blue tent appeared in the distance. She

suddenly sat forward, diverted from her ruminations, alert with interest. Jack steered the ship in the direction of the tent. As they closed in on it, it appeared to be big enough to hold six or seven people. It seemed so bizarre for it to be there, with nothing else around it.

The craft whirred to a stop in front of the tent. Jack and Kayla looked at each other, wondering what to do next. "If she really did just start walking, maybe someone here would have seen her," Kayla speculated.

"We should be careful," Jack cautioned as he climbed out. "We don't know who we'll find in there."

At that moment, the flap of the tent parted and a young woman about seventeen years old emerged. It took Kayla a few seconds to recognize her old friend, she was so changed. Amber's hair, once bleached silver and always worn in meticulously sculpted curls, was now wild and brown, and she had become excessively thin. But her distinctive huge blue eyes blinked into the sunlight, and her familiar smile spread across her face.

"Amber!" Kayla shouted, nearly tumbling out of the craft.

"Kayla? Oh, my God! It's you!"

Kayla grabbed her childhood friend in a tight hug. Tears of joy brimmed in her eyes.

When Amber pulled out of the hug, her face was also wet with happy tears. "How did you find me?"

she asked. "And leave it to you to show up in a *spaceship*. What's the deal with this?"

"It's an individual airborne transport," Kayla said, repeating Jack's words. "It's the next big thing." Kayla explained how they'd met with Aunt Emily, who'd pointed them in the right direction. She then told Amber how she'd driven out west with Dusa and how she was staying with the Drakians.

"Drakians!" Amber cried incredulously. "Do you actually know Drakians? I've heard of them. They sound so crazy. They worship that nutty neighbor of yours or something like that."

"We don't *worship* him, but we try to follow his example," Jack explained.

"What? You stink of Chinese cigarettes and scream at dogs?" Amber asked skeptically.

Kayla had missed the way Amber's outspokenness sometimes belied her warm heart. Even when they didn't agree, which was often, she always knew Amber was on her side.

"Drakians are active against the bar code tattoo," Kayla explained, "the way Gene Drake was active. He was strange, I know, but he took a stand."

"Whatever you say," Amber gave in, rolling her eyes. "You've always had a soft spot for oddballs and activists." Amber had never wanted her to get involved with Decode or the rebellion. Kayla thought it was ironic, considering how the bar code tattoo had ruined the Thorn family. The genetic imperfections revealed in their tattoos had sent them spiraling quickly to the bottom of society.

Amber threw her arms around Kayla again. "I'm just so happy to see you."

If Amber had been depressed, Kayla didn't see any sign of it now, though her expression grew serious. "Speaking of oddballs — you have to meet the lunatic who owns this tent. And there's something else. You're not going to believe it. I couldn't. But you've been on my mind all the time lately, and you'll know why the minute you go inside."

"What?" Kayla asked.

"See for yourself." Amber gestured for them to follow her into the tent. Food and water were laid out on a blanket by a sleeping bag, on which a teen-aged girl in camouflage-print shorts and a black sleeveless T-shirt lay sleeping on her back. Elab-orate, colorful, swirling tattoos were wrapped around her legs, arms, and chest. Her T-shirt had risen, exposing her midriff, which was also com-pletely covered with colorful ink designs. Even the sides of her neck and face boasted tattooed adorn-ments. There were designs of every kind: exotic birds, dragons, chains, barbed wire, waves, flowers dripping from heavy vines, angels, devils, dag-gers dripping blood, the moon and sun, skeletons, fire. And it all led to the black lines of her bar code tattoo, emblazoned on her forehead.

Kayla stared at the sleeping figure, fascination

mingled with confusion, even as some inner voice screamed at her to run.

It was not the macabre tattoo designs that held her so rapt. Another person might have missed the resemblance in the dazzle of vivid art surrounding the facial features. The dyed neon blue hair and heavily lined eyes could easily distract someone less intimately acquainted with the face than Kayla was. But she knew her own face well, and she saw it again facing her.

"It's you, isn't it?" Jack whispered, his voice filled with the same stunned amazement she felt.

Kayla nodded.

"He's final level," Amber whispered, once she and Kayla were again outside the tent.

"I know," Kayla agreed. Jack *was* handsome — spectacularly so — a fact that wouldn't be lost on Amber. But Kayla had other concerns at the moment.

"Listen," she said. "I need you to tell me how you got here and who this person is."

"I don't really know who she is. After Mom tried to burn off her tattoo and landed in the hospital, they held her there, saying she had TMP. So it was just Tarantula Woman and me — together and hating it. You can imagine — I was totally banged out. All I could do was take off or I would have totally lost it and become as freaky as she was."

Kayla nodded; her own harrowing meeting with

Aunt Emily had made Amber's point easy to understand. "How did you wind up *here*?" she asked.

"There was no one I could call to come get me," Amber explained. "So I just grabbed as much water as I could and headed into the desert. I walked until I conked out. When I woke up I was in this tent with Kendra. She found me and dragged me in. She lives out here alone. I've been with her ever since, about two weeks now."

"Haven't you noticed something about her?"

Amber's blue eyes widened as she nodded. "Of course I have! I'm not blind. That's why I said you've been on my mind lately. Remember? When I woke up in her tent at first I even thought it *was* you — that you'd gone completely wacko and covered yourself with all those tattoos. If you erased all that tattoo stuff, she could be your sister."

"Only I don't *have* a sister!" Kayla told Amber about meeting Kara and about Kara's vision of the palm reader who looked just like both of them. Then she recalled the frightening vision of the raving person in the desert. "I think that could have been Kendra," she said.

"It sure sounds like it was her," Amber agreed. "She's one sick ticket, but she has a reason to be."

"What's her deal?"

Before Amber could answer, Jack appeared at the tent flap. "Both of you should get out of the heat," he advised.

They followed him inside, where Kendra still

slept. “Kendra is writing a book about her life,” Amber told them in a whisper. “It’s some story, though I’m not sure if it’s true or if she’s making it all up. I think she wants me here so she can tell me what’s happened to her.”

“That’s insane. Why *are* you staying here?” Kayla asked.

Amber’s eyes widened, as if to say that the answer to that question should be obvious. “There are miles of endless nothing out there. I have *no* money and *no* family that’s still functioning. Where else am I going to go? It’s not like I have a single friend.” She paused, tilting her head thoughtfully. “It’s kind of ironic — don’t you think? — that the only person resembling a friend I wind up with out here is a twisted version of you, my best friend. Life is weird.”

“I can’t argue with that,” Jack put in with a sardonic laugh.

“Well, now I’m here. You’re coming with us,” Kayla told Amber firmly.

Amber smiled at her and nodded. “I’ve never tried to leave, so I don’t know how Kendra would feel about it. I’m not her prisoner or anything.” A puzzled expression came over her. “At least I don’t think I am. It’s possible, though. I guess I should wait for Kendra to wake up to say good-bye. It would be only decent since she *did* save my life — crazy or not.” She picked up a computer notebook that lay on the ground near Kendra and handed it to Kayla. "This is her story. I don't think she'd care if you read it, since she lets me see it. She works on it all night sometimes. That's why she's sleeping now."

Kayla switched on the notebook. The rectangular screen glowed to life as she sat on the blanket beside Jack where, together, they began reading it.

The Bizarre Story of Kendra Blake, the Avenging Spirit of the Desert

From the time of my birth on April 16, 2008, in Salt Lake City, Utah, I was aware that I was a freaked offshoot of the human strain. Unlike those around me. What else would explain the howling I've been told I incessantly inflicted on my devout Mormon parents? I suppose it was this assault on their ears that set them against me from the start. Other children stayed away as well, sensing I was not one of them.

Nobody likes me. Everybody hates me. I think I'll eat some worms. Big ones! Small ones! All kinds of different ones! Ones that squiggle and squirm!

As a young child I was excruciatingly aware of their eyes boring into my mind day and night, attempting to gaze into the depths of my thoughts in a futile attempt to know me. As if anyone could know me. I felt them, though, like fingers attempting to probe my psychic depths. Eventually I could bear their maddening stares no longer. Early one Sunday morning, I spread gasoline on the living room floor and tossed a lit match into it as I walked out the front door.

Fire! I bid you to burn!

I stood outside and watched. So pretty!

Shine, little glowworm, glimmer, glimmer.

My goal had been freedom, absolute autonomy. Instead, I was tossed into the Global-1 Center for Pediatric Rehabilitation.

I was seven.

The team of G-1 doctors and research scientists tried to conceal their glee at my arrival, covering it with murmurs of concern couched in pseudoscientific jargon, not realizing that I was wildly perceptive and heard the cackling of manic victory just beneath their facade of therapeutic crap. I had stumbled into their clutches and they were ecstatic.

Rehabilitation?

No.

Not that it would have been possible, but it was not even attempted.

Experimentation.

Mutilation.

Annihilation.

Those things were on the agenda at the Global-1 Center for Pediatric Rehabila-blah-blah. That was the prescribed course of care for Kendra Blake.

My parents' thought-probes were nothing compared with the instruments they used to test my mind. Daily, I was slathered with electrodes on every inch of my skin, medicated, subjected to strobe lights, shocks of every imaginable kind, and the surgeon's knife. This private torture chamber was my only home.

With puberty, the visions began.

At seventeen, the final indignity was forced upon me. They tied me down with nylon straps and inflicted their brand on me, making me no more than their cattle, one of their herd. They tattooed my wrist, but with a laser. I copied the bar code tattoo onto my forehead so all the world could see what they had done to me.

Their tests and experiments intensified. I felt no more human than the laboratory rats, the knockout mice they used for their other experimental abominations. And one day I learned that they saw me as no more human than those mice. Opening my file, I discovered that I had another name to them, an inhuman name.

I will write of my escape and how I scathed my skin, squeezing through the narrowest of cracks in a thick, outer wall, contorting my body until it writhed in agony and claustrophobic, breath-starved terror.

It didn't matter. I would have gnawed off my own arm like an animal in a trap to escape them.

In future writings, I will also tell how I learned to armor myself against them by inking my being with the protective totem symbols of the wide world, tattoos of my own choosing that would counter the shame of the bar code tattoo.

Images of the real world have power. The spirit world of the dead has power. The animal world has power. Images of these things I wear, and they empower me.

I am not an experiment. A mutilation. An annihilated freak.

I am art. I am the one with the bright plumage.

I am not KM-5, their name for me.

I am Kendra, the Avenging Spirit of the Desert.

The Phoenix.

The one who will not be caged.

CHAPTER 17

"Put that down!"

Startled, Kayla fumbled the computer notebook. Jack grabbed it before it hit the ground.

Kendra stood in front of them, her eyes ablaze with fury. "Who are you?" she demanded.

"They're my friends. I didn't think you'd mind," Amber explained nervously, stepping forward.

Kendra's eyes bored into Kayla. "You're one of us." She lunged for Kayla's arm and examined the fake tattoo on her wrist. "It's not real."

"Why do you think that?" Jack asked cautiously, keen to know what flaw she'd detected in his meticulously crafted fake.

She pointed to the bar code on her forehead. "The bars are wrong," she said, her voice angry. "Our bar codes are all the same."

"No, they're not," Kayla disagreed. "Every bar code is individual; all of them are different because they contain different information."

Kendra pushed her hard on the chest, sending Kayla sliding to the ground. "Moron! Idiot! Imbecile!" she screamed. "*Our* bar codes are *all* the same! Everyone else has an individual bar code, but *ours* are the same!"

"What do you mean, *ours*?" Kayla asked, staying on the ground, feeling safer there.

"Don't you know me? Don't you have the visions?" Kendra screamed.

"Hey, lay off her," Amber insisted boldly. "She has visions."

Jack extended his hand to help Kayla get up. "Visions? I know you're telepathic but . . . you see actual visions?"

"Sure!" Amber answered. "She's had them since we were about thirteen. We were at camp together when she saw a mental image of me nearly drowning in the lake. The next day it happened. I got a cramp while swimming. If she hadn't kept her eyes on me the whole time because she was worried about the vision, I would have drowned."

Kendra peered at her. "Then you must know. You must have seen me. I have seen you."

"I've seen you, too," Kayla admitted, slowly walking toward Kendra. "What are we to each other? Sisters? Cousins? Who was your mother?"

"My mother was not my mother," Kendra said, staring at Kayla with steely eyes. "And you are not my sister."

"What are you saying?" Kayla asked imploringly. "Do you know the answer to this?"

"My visions are the most powerful. Their experiments enhanced my ability more than any of you. I am the culmination of their efforts. My suffering at their hands has made me invulnerable, and there is no longer a need for the lesser selves!"

Kayla shrank back from Kendra, frightened by the maniacal gleam that had come into her eyes and the fervor of her words. What *others* was she talking about? What lesser selves?

"These tattoos armor me against them," Kendra continued her rant. "I have eluded capture and in so doing have transformed into a new creature, one who can outwit and intimidate." As she raved on, she lifted her arms. Kayla noticed that the undersides of both of them were tattooed with feathers, a gorgeous pattern of blue, green, and brown. Wings!

With her arms still raised, Kendra turned, displaying the feathered tattoo that extended all the way to the two protruding wing bones of her muscular upper back. "I am a being of the future!" she shouted. "I cannot be bound to this desultory, mundane plane of existence." This was the voice Kayla had heard in her vision, the same monomaniacal, enraged ranting.

"Who are the others?" Kayla dared to ask.

Kendra swung around to face her directly, stepping in front of her and speaking aggressively in Kayla's face. "You are KM-1. The thief is KM-2. The corporate fool is KM-3. The palm reader is KM-4. At each step they added more and more power. I have seen you all because I am KM-5."

"Who is KM-6?" Kayla asked, remembering the file on Grandma Cathy. "I read a file that talked about KM-1-6."

"We are all KM, one to six! But KM-6 is dead! They tried to surpass my power, to fly higher. But like Icarus who fell from the sky, they overreached themselves."

"Do we have the same mother?" Kayla pressed, frightened but desperate to know.

Leaping forward, Kendra abruptly yanked Kayla's hair and, in a flurry of agile movement, drew a switchblade from her back pocket. "Our mother is us and I am her perfection. All the lesser selves must die! I will not rest until I am all that remains."

Kendra raised the knife to Kayla's throat — but in the next second, Amber twisted the arm away and sent Kendra staggering back.

Whirling around, infuriated, Kendra knocked Amber to the ground. Still clutching her switchblade, she lunged at Kayla again.

This time, Jack jumped between them and landed a punch directly to her jaw. Kendra stumbled but recovered instantly, returning the punch and connecting squarely with his nose, sending blood streaming from it.

Just as Kendra prepared for another punch, Kayla swept up Jack's pack and swung it at Kendra, hitting the side of her head.

As Kendra careened, flailing for balance, Amber, Kayla, and Jack darted outside the tent and leaped into the swing-lo. Amber squeezed between Jack and Kayla, sitting on the back ledge of the two-seater craft. Jack activated the control panel, his hands flying with lightning speed. The craft lifted just as Kendra burst from the tent, eyes ablaze and waving her knife.

Kayla grabbed Amber's hand to steady her as Jack brought the craft to full speed. In minutes, they'd put a good distance between themselves and Kendra.

Jack slowed the swing-lo. "Everybody okay?"

Kayla and Amber nodded.

"Well, that was not like anything I ever expected to happen," Jack remarked, turning the craft in the direction of the cave. "How on earth were you living with that lunatic, Amber?"

"Honestly, I never saw her as banged out as she was today," Amber insisted convincingly. "From the moment she saw Kayla she got extra flippy."

"I wonder what kinds of experiments they did to her," Kayla said. Despite Kendra's bizarre, aggressive behavior, Kayla felt sympathy for her. Perhaps it was hard not to feel for someone who gazed at her with her own eyes. It was as though Kara and Kendra were living alternate realities. They were like Kayla, but surviving under vastly different circumstances, their personalities shaped by different events and different environments.

Kayla felt powerfully connected to all of them. Even Kendra, murderous maniac though she was, was only trying to survive. Somehow, Kayla felt she understood her struggle.

CHAPTER 18

Back at the cave, the Drakians welcomed Amber and were fascinated to hear her story of how the bar code tattoo had destroyed her life.

"I wonder what's wrong with your codes?" Nate said.

"Bipolar disorder," Amber replied. "Aunt Emily made me suspect it, and when I asked, my dad admitted that it runs all through my family. My mother's side is full of Parkinson's disease."

"But they cured Parkinson's with stem cell therapy years ago," Kayla pointed out.

"Doesn't matter," said Dusa. "They don't even want to be bothered treating it. They'd rather eliminate people with the disease than pay for their treatment."

Kayla had been standing nearby listening when she suddenly felt limp with fatigue. Jack noticed her leaning against the cave wall, her arm extended for support, and joined her. "You'd better lie down," he suggested, gently touching her shoulder. "You were pumped with adrenaline; now you're feeling the letdown. Plus, that desert sun can wipe you out. I should build some kind of roof on the swing-lo for shelter."

He grabbed a sleeping bag from a storage trunk and led her to the back cavern where the stalactites and stalagmites were so abundant. "It's quiet and cool in here," he said, spreading out the bag. "You should rest."

Kayla did feel wiped. She stretched out on the bag and shut her eyes. Sleep didn't come immediately, but instead she rested in a semiwaking state, aware of the slow drip sound coming from somewhere in the cave. Its repetitive steadiness was soothing. . . .

* * *

She is in a black room. Outside are the crashing waves of a vast and tumultuous ocean. In dim light she is looking at a hand. A voice says, "It's up to you to stop this. Help will be called from the sky, though I do not know if it will come in time to save us all." A right hand traces the line of a palm on another right hand. She recognizes the hands, the slim fingers, the curve of the palm. Both of them are her own.

* * *

With a shudder, Kayla awakened from her trance.

Two right hands? she wondered.

* * *

Later that evening, Kayla walked out in the desert with Jack. "Do you think the swing-lo could get us to California?" she asked.

"Don't know. I'd be interested in testing it, though. California isn't that far. Why do you want to go there?"

"I had a . . . a . . . vision."

"Oh, right. Your psychic visions," Jack said.

"Yeah. I think I was born with some natural ability but I got better at it during the time I spent studying in the Adirondacks with Eutonah. She's a powerful shaman. Even now, she can project her spirit out of her body and travel."

"Astral projection," he said. "My grandmother in Ireland claimed she could do it."

"Did you believe her?"

"Hey, did anyone ever think I'd be zipping around the desert like George Jetson?" he replied. "I think anything's possible."

His words brought back a memory of Allyson's last letter to August, the one where she said the same thing: *Anything is possible.*

"I'd like to go see my friend Allyson at Caltech in Pasadena," Kayla told Jack. "And I had a vision that I believe was of the person Kendra called KM-4, the palm reader. In the vision, she was reading my palm. She told me help would come to me from the sky."

They had walked far enough from the cave that their only light was a blanket of stars. He knelt and took matches from his back pocket to light a tangle of dry sagebrush that had slowly tumbled toward them. It burst into flame instantly.

A distant look came into his eyes, as though he was calculating something. "I wish I knew how high the swing-lo can fly. Maybe if I get it going I'll be the one who's able to help you."

"Why don't you test it?" she suggested. "The desert seems like the perfect place."

He stared into the steadily glowing fire of the tumbleweed. "I'm afraid of heights," he revealed, a note of embarrassment in his voice.

"The fire walk didn't cure you of your fears?" she asked gently.

He smiled sadly, still staring into the fire. "Do you know why your feet didn't burn?"

Kayla shook her head. She assumed it had something to do with mind over matter — but otherwise she had no idea.

"Most people don't know, so when they do the walk it takes enormous courage. But before *my* walk, I already knew that ash is an excellent insulator. The heat from the coals doesn't travel through it easily. If the fire has been burning long enough and there is a good layer of ash covering the coal bed, you won't get burned as long as you keep moving quickly. The ash is like a blanket of protection over the coals."

"I had no idea," Kayla admitted. "So you're saying that you didn't get the benefit from it because you already knew you could do it?"

"Right. If I take the swing-lo high into the air, *that* would be overcoming my greatest fear. To help you, I might be able to do it. I'd be willing to try, anyway."

She looked at him there in the flickering light and their eyes met. She knew he was acknowledging the feeling that had been silently growing between them, a strong attraction that was both physical and emotional. She felt a powerful urge to kiss him — it would have been the most natural thing to do at that moment. But she also thought of Mfumbe, trapped in his bed by sickness and injury — her Mfumbe, who had gone through so much to stand by her.

This thought made her refrain from the kiss, offering only a warm smile instead. Still, she wondered how much longer she could keep herself from moving into his arms.

PART 3

To every man is given the key
to the gates of heaven;
the same key opens the gates of hell.

Buddhist proverb quoted by
Richard Feynman in his talk titled
"The Value of Science"

CHAPTER 19

The swing-lo hovered low to the ground and then descended to a stop on a grassy mall on the campus of the California Institute of Technology. Jack had driven it much like a car, keeping it only several feet above the ground the entire way. Because they'd stayed so low, they'd expected their landing to go unnoticed, but Kayla and Jack were instantly surrounded by keen-eyed, fascinated students who had immediately identified the craft as aerodynamic. As one of the premier centers for scientific research in the country, Caltech attracted some of the best and brightest students. "I hope you have a patent on this, man," said one student as he rubbed his hands along the swing-lo's sides.

"Sure I do," Jack said as they climbed out, though Kayla had the feeling it wasn't so.

"Who's your sponsor, what company?" asked a young woman.

"Don't say it's G-1, please," said a young man with a bald head.

"Who else would it be?" Jack bluffed with a convincing confidence.

"One of the small start-up companies," yet another young male student suggested.

"Naw," Jack said dismissively. "None of them can match G-1 for manufacturing. These crafts are the next big thing and whoever can produce them the cheapest is going to corner the market. You have to go with G-1 or you're sunk before you start." These remarks were met with a mix of resigned agreement and grumbling.

"Anybody know where I can find a Professor Gold, the nanobot guy?" Jack asked the crowd . . . and it seemed that just about everyone knew.

As Jack took down the directions to Professor Gold's office, Kayla marveled at how convincing his bluff about Global-1 had been. It brought back unsettling memories of how Zekeal had concealed from her his true involvement with Global-1 and his ties to Tattoo Gen.

She pushed her doubts aside; of course they had to seem to be on board with Global-1. They were wearing fake bar code tattoos — Dusa had given her a fake containing Kathryn Reed's file. "When you lie about something it's good to stay as close to the truth as you can," she'd reasoned as she pressed it onto Kayla's wrist. Kayla found it eerie to be pretending to be her own grandmother.

Jack grabbed Kayla's hand. "Come on. We're close." They hurried along the walkway to a brick building with large picture windows and entered it. Professor Gold's office was listed on the information board as being on the third floor, so they took the elevator up.

Before they reached Professor Gold's office, they passed a large glassed-in room crammed with computers and printers spitting out yards of paper containing bar graphs. "There she is!" Kayla cried softly, spotting Allyson behind one of them. Excited, she banged on the glass.

Allyson looked to the sound and her face instantly lit up with delighted recognition. Her appearance was nearly the same as Kayla remembered. The halo of messy blond curls that always surrounded her round, angelic face was now pushed up onto the top of her head and held in place with a pencil. Kayla thought it looked slightly blonder. Her pale skin was now the golden color of a lightly toasted marshmallow, which gave her an outdoorsy look she'd never had before. A white lab coat replaced the loosely flowing tops she used to favor to cover the fifteen or so extra pounds she wanted to lose, so it was hard to be certain but it seemed that she had shed at least some of them. She was still Allyson, but her looks were somewhat improved.

She waved them inside and then met Kayla with a heartfelt hug, which Kayla returned. It was so good to see her old friend again. When they separated, Allyson glanced at Kayla's wrist and her eyes widened in horror at the sight of the fake bar code tattoo.

Kayla mouthed the word *fake,* and Allyson instantly relaxed.

Jack, who had been hanging back by the door, stepped forward, and Kayla introduced him. Allyson shook his hand but looked worried. "Where's Mfumbe?" she asked.

Kayla told her what had happened. It was a story Jack was hearing for the first time, too, and he listened with rapt attention.

"Poor Mfumbe. He must feel so trapped," Allyson sympathized.

"Right now he *is* trapped," Kayla agreed. "He's trapped by the injuries he suffered and by his parents. Dusa and I brought him there because he was badly hurt, but now I'm not sure we did the right thing."

"If he was spitting up blood he most likely had internal bleeding. That's serious — you did the right thing," Allyson said.

"The worst of it is the bar code tattoo they forced on him," Kayla told her. "I've been in touch with him and he's really depressed."

"I guess August was depressed after the march, too, even though he wasn't caught," Allyson said. "I wish I'd been in closer touch with him."

"I wish I had, too," Kayla agreed, feeling again the sting of guilt about not having been more aggressive in her efforts to contact August.

"I can't believe that out of our whole group, you're the only one of us left who isn't bar-coded," Allyson pointed out sadly. "I guess I really owe you an apology. When you first came to our resistance meeting with Zekeal, I thought you were nice but I also assumed you were this ditzy, artsy girl who would get a bar code as soon as things got rough. I figured you were just after Zekeal. But as it turns out, you're the strongest of us all. Look how you've managed to keep ahead of G-1 and how you've been brave enough not to give in all this time."

Kayla had never thought of herself as strong, or even particularly bright or brave. In her own eyes, she was just a girl, more average than anything else, doing her best to figure things out and keep going.

"She's amazing," Jack chimed in.

"You guys are nice," Kayla said, brushing them off. Wanting to get the focus off herself, she walked farther into the room to the computers and printers. "What is all this stuff?" she asked.

"We're studying biological applications for nanotechnology — nanobiotechnology," Allyson explained, and gave them a tour of the research facility. "We're working with our infometrics department to —"

"Infometrics?" Kayla interrupted. "What's that?"

"It's a field of study that merges genetics with computer analysis," Allyson explained. "All these computers and printers are gathering and reporting on every bit of available data on government and private genetic experimentation in the field of genetic engineering. We have the most advanced equipment here."

She pointed to a board with dots of colorful lights on it. "That's a machine that constantly runs a DNA microarray and projects the results onto a screen. The DNA microarray has been around since 2001, but this computer streamlines the process, running the tests and reporting results instantly. It can tell us what genes are active in an organism and give us a visual snapshot of the cell's genetic script."

"You're losing me," Kayla warned, with a self-conscious laugh at her own lack of scientific knowledge.

Allyson smiled. "All you really need to know is that it helps us compare the genetic contents of a healthy cell with that of a diseased cell. When it first came out, this thing helped researchers to understand how the AIDS virus replicated. Through the years it's become more and more sophisticated."

"What are all these printouts?" Jack asked.

"Dr. Gold is searching for information that will enable him to put his new virus-fighting nanobots to their best use."

"How much access do they have?" Jack asked.

"They're searching worldwide data banks for information, but it's been difficult since these global companies aren't always eager to share what they know.

"I call this main computer Helen of Troy because she's capable of launching a thousand programs,"

Allyson said with a grin. She then took a step closer to them and bent her head away from the other researchers working in the room. "I'd like to show you guys something I've uncovered. I'm so glad you're here, because there's no one else I would trust with this."

Her words sent a chill through Kayla, who looked around the room to check if they were being observed. Everyone appeared to be going about their business, uninterested in the three of them.

Allyson stepped away again and took on a more normal attitude. "Here are the keys to my apartment. I'll be there as soon as I can and we'll catch up. I live off campus. I'll write down my address."

Kayla took the keys from her as they walked back to the door. "It's so great to see you," she said animatedly, leaning in for another parting hug.

As they embraced, Allyson whispered into Kayla's ear. "I have another set of keys for myself. Keep the door locked and don't let anyone in."

The swing-lo's built-in global positioning tracker made it easy for them to find where Allyson lived. "Where will I park this thing?" Jack wondered as they hovered outside the low apartment building just minutes from the institute.

"Park it on the roof," Kayla suggested.

Jack eyed the three-story climb nervously. "No," he decided. Hitting some buttons, he tilted the craft until it was nearly at a ninety-degree angle and sent it forward. Kayla gripped its sides anxiously as he drove it through a narrow opening between the building and a chain-link fence, quickly coming out to a grassy yard behind the apartment. "This will do," he said, climbing out.

Back in front, they used Allyson's keys to let themselves in the front door. The building was old, from the early twentieth century, they guessed.

"I've been thinking about the Helen of Troy computer," Jack said quietly in the shadowy front hall. "You know those computer algorithms I was telling you about, the ones that might reveal what Gene Drake knew?"

Kayla nodded. "Uh-huh." The algorithms were the key to unlocking the information that would tell them what terrible secret was stored in the bar code tattoo, the secret so much worse even than the accumulation of genetic histories.

"I want to talk to Allyson about the possibility of using Helen of Troy to hack into the G-1 files and get those codes," he said as they climbed the narrow stairs to the apartment on the third floor.

Kayla realized that she'd be alone there with Jack. Except when they had been together in the swing-lo or walking in the desert, this hadn't occurred before. Now they were someplace private, and she was suddenly nervous about what might happen. She trusted him to respect her wishes — she just wasn't entirely certain of what those wishes were. She was promising herself she'd be loyal to Mfumbe, and she was picturing herself with Jack at the same time. It wasn't a vision of any kind, simply her imagination wandering into dangerous territory.

The spacious, sunny, one-room apartment was at the end of a long hall. They entered and Kayla immediately sank into the soft futon couch. It had been a long time since she'd experienced any of the comforts of everyday life. Shutting her eyes, she let the softness of the cushion surround her. "Allyson must have a shower here," she suddenly realized. After months of washing in streams, lakes, and public restrooms, a shower seemed like an unbelievable luxury.

Jack tossed her a towel he found in a closet. "You go first. Then me."

Kayla washed her hair with Allyson's lavender-scented shampoo and luxuriated in the flow of warm water down her back. As she soaped herself she was once again reminded of how hard her muscles had become and how calloused her feet were from the tough life she'd been living. When she was done, she threw her shorts, T-shirt, and underwear into the tub and watched the filthy water run into the drain.

She was toweling her hair dry when Jack knocked. "One minute," she called as she scrambled to wrap herself in the towel. It was barely tucked into place when he came in wearing only a towel around his waist.

A moment charged with mutual attraction followed as they looked at each other. He stepped closer so that his face was only inches from hers. She ached to reach for him, to feel his lips on hers.

"You're not ready for this, are you?" he asked, realizing the moment was thick with possibility but that she was hesitant.

"Are you?" she asked back.

He smiled. "Just say the word and I'm ready."

She nodded, smiling at him despite her concerns. "I have someone special," she said. "I wouldn't like it if he went with someone else."

"He's far away . . . and things change," he said.

The front door creaked as it was opened. "Hello?"

"Allyson's here," Kayla said, realizing she was relieved that the moment had been broken by her friend's arrival. Pulling her towel tighter, she went out to greet her, leaving Jack in the bathroom.

Allyson tossed her jam-packed bag on the futon and grabbed a bottled iced tea from the refrigerator. "Everything okay?" she asked.

"Just showering," Kayla replied, taking an iced tea from her. "I didn't think you would mind."

"Not at all. Are you still with Mfumbe?"

Kayla smiled but sighed with exasperation. "Yeah."

"He'd be pretty hard to resist," she commented, nodding toward the shower sounds coming from the bathroom.

Kayla rolled her eyes and laughed. "He's a good guy, too. I'm hanging tough, though. After everything Mfumbe and I have gone through together, I owe him that much."

"Loyalty is important," Allyson agreed, "especially nowadays when you don't know who to trust. But you and Mfumbe haven't made any promises, have you?"

"No. It's just understood," Kayla replied.

Allyson shrugged. "Fortunately — or unfortunately — right now I don't have to worry about those kinds of problems. I have other things that are obsessing me."

Allyson took a billowy sundress from her closet and tossed it to Kayla. It hung like a tent on Kayla until Allyson directed her to a belt in the top drawer.

The shower stopped, and in a few minutes Jack emerged, dressed just in his shorts. "That felt good," he commented with a smile. "What is it you were going to show us, Allyson?"

Without answering him, Allyson moved purposefully toward the back wall of the apartment. Kneeling, she dug her fingertips into a thin groove in the hardwood floor and easily pried up a plank that had clearly already been loosened. A satisfied smile spread across her face. "This is what I wanted you to see," she said, peeling off an e-chip taped to the plank's underside.

Digging in her purse, she took out her handheld

computer and loaded the chip. "I don't know if anyone realizes it, even Dr. Gold, but his data-collecting computers are almost *too* powerful. They were designed by a real genius, a student in the infometrics department, and when they encounter a program they can't open, they act like hackers, breaking into systems that are heavily password-protected."

"I wish I'd invented that," Jack said, his voice oozing respect.

"Tell me about it," Allyson agreed. "And get this — the real reason I call that main computer Helen of Troy is because I think it might even contain a Trojan-horselike program that collects log-ins and passwords as it runs. Helen of Troy gains root access to other computers in a way I've never seen. Somehow it even got into a file protected with both voice *and* radio frequency identification systems."

"That's crazy, final level," Jack murmured, obviously very impressed.

"No kidding. When I saw the file I'm about to show you, I knew it had to be highly classified. I grabbed it before anyone else saw it. I'm not sure why, exactly."

"When you do things instinctively it usually seems to be the right thing to do," Kayla commented.

"I guess so. I didn't know what else to do. I'm not sure what Dr. Gold's politics are. So much research here has Global-1 backing, even though they hide behind the smaller companies they own. A lot of the time the scientists doing the research don't even realize they're working for Global-1."

"You got it all on an e-chip?" Jack questioned.

"Two e-chips," she said. "It's a massive file full of subdirectories. I loaded the subs onto a chip that I have hidden somewhere else. I thought it would be best to keep them separate."

She flipped on the speaker. A robotic voice read out loud the words that appeared in the monitor window.

"Wait until you get a load of this," Allyson said as the robotic voice began.

Kayla and Jack listened, spellbound by what they were hearing.

REPORT ON GLOBAL-1 NANOBIOTECHNOLOGY PROGRAMS

Global-1 has been in the vanguard of cloning advances since the turn of the century when it became the majority shareholder in every major biotech company in the Western world and large parts of Asia. Its two main branches are known as AgroGlobal and GlobalHelix.

AgroGlobal was largely responsible for exerting the influence needed to shift the world's food supply over to 100 percent genetically altered produce by the year 2018. GlobalHelix was originally founded in 2006 as an adjunct to AgroGlobal. Its stated purpose at the time of its creation was the genetic enhancement of livestock for consumption as food and for breeding. It relied heavily on the pioneering cloning techniques of Dr. Ian Wilmut in the previous century.

GlobalHelix later became a pioneer in the field of splicing genes to create transgenic animals. These were first developed using mice, through a microinjection of DNA into the nucleus of the egg. The ability to add genes to an organism has been instrumental in the study of human disease. It also has other practical applications. For example, the milk of livestock can be genetically altered to contain large amounts of pharmaceutically valuable proteins such as insulin or factor VIII for treating sick humans. A human gene such as that of insulin when expressed in the mammary glands of a sheep was found to be a breakthrough treatment for diabetes patients in 2014.

This biotechnical therapy was quickly rendered obsolete by the development of insulin-releasing nanopores in 2015. Advances in molecular-size robotics created this breakthrough wherein specially programmed nanobots were injected into the bloodstream where they released insulin at regular intervals. The financial blow this dealt to GlobalHelix proved temporary since GlobalHelix was able to acquire the company responsible for the insulin-issuing nanobots. From 2015 on, GlobalHelix has invested heavily in nanobiotechnology research and development.

Another major area of interest for GlobalHelix was the development of transgenic animals for organ transplant into humans. They were the first to successfully splice human genes into pigs to create organs for human transplant. Problems of organ harvesting were eliminated by using pigs as donors, and the problem of organ rejection was overcome by splicing human genes into pig organs. This scientific breakthrough enabled GlobalHelix to have laws prohibiting cloning and gene splicing overturned by the beginning of 2020.

GlobalHelix has moved rapidly into the exciting world of human cloning since 2020. Its worldwide companies — Global-2 in Japan, Global-3 in Brazil, Global-4 in Mexico, and Global-5 in France — have been able to circumvent U.S. restrictions on human experimentation by moving their research to countries with less stringent laws.

Ongoing programs being carried out by the Global-1 parent company and its offshoots are listed below. These links can only be opened by radio frequency authentication and eye scan, followed by voice recognition.

- Nuclear Transfer Cloning for Livestock
- Potential Applications in Cell-based Therapies
- Pre- and Perinatal Mortality in Cloned Organisms
- Applications of Nanobiotechnology (see further links below)
- Production of Identical Sextuplet Humans During the First Cell Cycle of Nuclear DNA Transfer

CHAPTER 20

"What's going on with the nanobots?" Jack asked.

"Smart! You zeroed right in on it," Allyson commended him. "As you know, to call something nano means it's measured in billionths of a meter, which is just about the same size as a molecule. Since the mid-1980s, scientists have talked about constructing self-replicating nanomachines that could assemble atoms into molecules. It's the same thing that living cells do naturally."

"So they're mechanical cells?" Kayla asked.

"Basically, yeah. Cells are like living nanobots. Nanobots are similar in size to molecular proteins and DNA. They can be engineered to have specific or multiple functions. If you inject a person with a nanobot, the bot could analyze a cell's contents and send the information back to a microarray machine like you saw today. It could also deliver drugs or destroy a cancerous cell."

Kayla's father had once shown her an old Pac-Man game from his childhood. Kayla remembered the aggressive dot gobbling up everything in its path and imagined it was a nanobot destroying living cells it didn't approve of.

"This is the part that bothers me," Allyson said

as she activated the Applications of Nanobiotechnology link. Several subheads appeared under a heading marked HIGHLY CLASSIFIED.

- Propeace12 Release
- Vagus Nerve Stimulator Release
- Vagus Nerve Stimulator Intensified Release
- BC12 Virus Release
- Program Activation Dates

"My mother was addicted to Propeace just before she died," Kayla recalled. Mrs. Reed had taken the powerful tranquilizer with increasing frequency after Kayla's father died, and many days she'd seemed like a zombie wandering around in a trance.

"What's a vagus nerve stimulator?" Jack asked.

"I did some research when I saw this link and discovered that back in 1997 a company came out with a device to help patients who had epilepsy. It was surgically implanted in the upper chest, and its wires were threaded through the patient's neck to send timed electrical pulses to stimulate the vagus nerve leading to the brain. In 2006 it was approved for treating patients with severe depression."

"Did it work?" Kayla asked.

"Yes and no. Some people liked it and claimed they felt better. Other patients felt no difference and complained that it put a quiver or a rumble in their voices. It was discontinued in 2022 after gene therapy cured epilepsy and they came out with the new genetic antidepressant drugs."

"Let's get into the link and see what our pals at Global-1 are up to," Jack suggested.

"Can't," Allyson told him. "My handheld won't open these links. They have yet another level of eye scan security on them."

"Can the superinfometric computers handle it?" he asked.

"I'm not sure," Allyson replied. "I don't know if they can break through an eye scan. Even if we could get them to open the files, it would be tricky to do it without everyone else in the laboratory seeing."

"What happens there at night?" he asked.

"I have a key, but it would be suspicious if I used it in the middle of the night. Security would inform Dr. Gold, and I'd have to explain."

They walked together down to the Caltech campus. Along the way, Jack told Allyson about the secret algorithms he was trying to uncover. She agreed that Helen of Troy might be able to locate the codes, but they had to tell it where to look first. The supercomputer was accessing such a high volume of information that even if it did feed the algorithm codes to them they might not be able to sift through the mass of data in time to realize they'd received the codes. "We have to narrow and isolate its search," Allyson said.

They reached the building where Allyson did her research in Dr. Gold's facility. She walked in alone and spoke to the guard at the front desk, claiming to have left an important book upstairs. He said he would like to let her in and would even go with her, but he was alone for the rest of the week since the other guard, his partner, was out sick. His being alone meant he couldn't leave the front desk.

Out of luck, Kayla, Jack, and Allyson went back to the apartment without much conversation, each seeming wrapped in a private concern. Kayla guessed Jack was working on getting them into that building the following night. Maybe Allyson was going over the information she had, trying to make sense of it. She might even be thinking about the question Jack had posed to her — how to find the secret bar code algorithms.

Kayla knew what was absorbing *her* mind. She couldn't stop thinking about the G-1 project Allyson had stumbled upon titled: Production of Identical Sextuplet Humans During the First Cell Cycle of Nuclear DNA Transfer.

Kathryn Marie Reed had had a child called KM-1-6.

Sextuplets?

It was nearly two in the morning when Allyson used the remote to shut the wide-screen TV that hung flat against the wall. "That is too banged out," she said as the screen went black. The public service announcement that featured the Kayla look-alike, the one claiming to be Kayla, had just been on. "It's obviously a digital fake."

"Maybe," Kayla allowed. "That's what Mfumbe thought, too."

In an overstuffed chair in a corner, Jack mumbled in his sleep and flung his hand over the arm of the chair.

"Why do you say *maybe*?" Allyson asked as she rummaged in her freezer until she produced a quart of chocolate ice cream and then stuck two spoons into it. She brought it back to the futon couch and offered Kayla one of the spoons. Kayla gratefully accepted it.

She told Allyson about meeting Kara and Kendra, and of her vision of the palm reader with hands so much like her own.

"Have you opened the link about the sextuplets?" she asked Allyson.

Allyson immediately realized what Kayla was thinking and sat there a moment, spoon still in her mouth, pondering it. "Let's look now," she said, going for her handheld computer on a nearby table.

With Kayla watching over her shoulder, she activated the link. Quickly, they began reading. Kayla didn't understand much of what she saw. It talked about how DNA was the molecular basis of genes and how DNA fragments containing genes could be copied in a host cell, usually a bacterium. The genetic makeup of the resulting cloned cells was called a cell line and was identical to the original cell. Then it went on to talk about somatic cells and germ cells. She read phrases such as: *Mammalian differences are achieved by systematic changes in gene expression brought about by interactions between the nucleus and the changing cytoplasmic environment,* which eluded her completely.

After a few minutes more of reading text that was mostly incomprehensible to her, Kayla stopped, bewildered. Allyson read on before she finally lifted her head and stared at Kayla. "You know what this all comes down to, don't you?" she asked.

Kayla shook her head. "I'm not exactly sure," she admitted.

"Cloning."

Kayla stared back at her as the meaning of this sank in. "But there's no reason to think this has anything to do with me, right?"

"I read ahead and I found something interesting," Allyson said. "Was anyone in your family named Kathryn Marie Reed?"

Kayla's eyes darted to the bottom of the screen. As with the nanobiotechnology section, there were additional links marked HIGHLY CLASSIFIED. They named different experiments and gave the names of the people involved in them. She scanned them rapid-fire until she came to the line that stopped her cold:

- Genetic Enhancement/Manipulation Program: Donor Kathryn Marie Reed

Ocean waves crashed into the nearby shore. A full moon illuminated the scene in wavering silver light. Kayla was walking along the beach when she saw a dark, moving line approaching.

A line of people was walking toward the water. Their hair was on fire. But they didn't seem to care. They stared straight ahead, progressing steadily toward the waves.

Mfumbe was in the line, the top of his head ablaze, his eyes fixed blankly ahead. Kayla ran to him but he didn't recognize her. "It's me," she cried, shaking his arm as if to wake him from his trance. "Don't you know me?"

He turned and she saw that Kara and Kendra were behind him in the line. Farther back, a third figure and fourth figure had her form and hair, but their faces were a blur.

The line passed her by as they walked into the ocean, quickly disappearing between the silvered waves. Mfumbe was up to his shoulders, about to disappear below the water, too. Crashing through the surf, she grabbed his arm. "Stop!" she shouted.

For a moment he seemed to recognize her. "Kayl-l-l-a?" The line of drowning figures echoed his words. "Kayl-l-l-a!" The drawn out, repeated l spread across the moving ocean until it was amplified into a wild, wind-borne ululation.

The line continued on into the sea. Mfumbe was in water up to his chin now. She had to swim to reach him. "Stop!" she screamed as she splashed through the churning water. "Stop! All of you, stop!"

"Kayla, wake up! Wake up!" Her eyes snapped open and she gazed up at Jack sitting beside her on the futon couch, his face silver with the moonlight coming in through the window. "You were dreaming and yelling 'stop' in your sleep."

With a shudder, she sat up and remembered the dream. It had been so frightening. Tears sprang to her eyes.

He put his arm around her, pulling her closer. She rested her head on his chest.

It felt so safe to have his arms around her, so good. But she was glad Allyson was asleep on the pullout sofa just yards away, preventing anything further from happening . . . for now.

CHAPTER 21

"How far is Los Angeles from here?" Kayla asked Allyson in the morning.

"Just twelve miles," Allyson replied from the kitchen, where she was buttering toast for their breakfast. "Why?"

"My grandmother died in a psychiatric institution there. I thought I'd go search around and see what I can find out about her."

"It's a big city," Allyson cautioned.

Jack picked up Allyson's handheld computer. "Maybe I can save some legwork by running a few preliminary searches," he said, stretching out on the futon and beginning to input information.

Kayla joined Allyson at the table. "I was hoping you and Jack could come to the facility with me today," Allyson said. "Together we might be able to figure out a way to get the infometric computers to open those subfiles. We could search for the secret bar code algorithms, too."

"Final level!" Jack burst out triumphantly, swinging around and off the futon. "I found your grandmother! What a hacker genius I am!"

"If you say so yourself," Allyson teased.

“I do say it,” he said, unabashedly proud. His search had connected the name Kathryn Reed to a private psychiatric facility in Los Angeles. It had once been called St. Francis Clinic but was then taken over by Global-1 and renamed the GlobalHelix Mental Health Center.

By cracking their security code, he’d entered a subfile that gave him an index of former patients in which he found Kathryn Reed’s name. “It looks as though she was in and out of there a number of times between 2007 and 2015,” he reported, reading the information on the screen.

“What does it say about her mental illness?”

Jack looked up from the computer with a puzzled expression. “Nothing.”

“What do you mean?” Kayla asked.

“It says she was admitted to the center for treatment of schizophrenia, but everything in this file has to do with her DNA.” He continued to read rapidly, his eyes darting across the screen. “It says she donated genetic material for ‘cellular experimentation.’”

Allyson joined Jack on the futon and read the screen with him, her expression becoming increasingly troubled.

“Tell me,” Kayla pressed anxiously.

“I don’t think your grandmother really *was* schizophrenic,” Allyson said. “To me, it looks like that was just a cover story to conceal the real reason she was there.”

"I don't get it."

"Kayla, I don't know how to say this," Allyson said. "So I'll just come out with it. It looks like you're a clone of your grandmother. She was selling her genetic material to Global-1 for a cloning project."

"Which means she's not actually your grandmother," Jack added gently. "Your great-grandmother would be your mother. Kathryn Marie Reed is your . . . twin, I suppose."

Allyson nodded. "Twins — or triplets or quadruplets or quintuplets — are the closest thing in nature to clones."

"But clones have no father?" Kayla asked, barely speaking through her shock.

"Genetically speaking, your great-grandfather provided the male component in your creation. Kathryn Reed's father is also your biological father. They replicated Kathryn's DNA however many times."

"Six times," Kayla said slowly, remembering the name of Kathryn Reed's child as it was listed in her file.

KM-1-6.

Saying she needed a little time alone, Kayla left the apartment and began to walk. She had so much to think about.

A clone. She was an identical genetic copy of someone else — of Kathryn Marie Reed.

So much made sense now. Kara. Kendra. The palm reader. The smiling, bar-code-loving Kayla on the TV. Kayla herself. And the one Kendra had said was dead — KM-6.

This had so many meanings for her. Her parents were not her parents. It meant her father was her older brother, in a way. No — it made her *his* aunt, his mother's sister. At least it meant they were related.

She laughed, darkly remembering how everyone had always commented that she resembled her father but was the exact image of her late grandmother. No kidding!

She did some calculating. Kathryn Reed would have been forty-nine years old in 2008, the year Kayla was born. A little old to give birth but not impossible, though maybe she hadn't given birth. The embryos might have been implanted in different mothers.

Kayla had once had pictures of her mother sitting in a hospital bed holding her as a newborn. And she'd seen pictures of her mother when she was pregnant. So her mother, Ashley Reed, must have been carrying her own mother-in-law's clone.

Why had they done it? Was it for money? Her father had worked for the FBI. What if it was part of some government experiment?

Kayla recalled something that made her stop walking, stunned by the realization. The night before, the file Allyson had showed them had listed Kathryn Reed as a participant in the Genetic Enhancement/Manipulation Program.

Enhancement and *manipulation.*

There were six clones, and GlobalHelix had done something to change their genes.

Kendra in all her ranting madness had talked about an increasing level of enhanced powers. When she had been in the G-1 Pediatric Rehabilitation Center she'd glimpsed her own GlobalHelix file. Is that what she'd learned — that each cloned embryo had been enhanced at an increasingly intensified level? Enhanced how?

They had to get the infometric computers to open the subfiles. They needed to know what other experiments GlobalHelix was doing with nanobiotechnology. And she needed to learn exactly what they had done to her genes.

She hurried back to Allyson's apartment, eager to talk with her friends about what she'd been thinking. She had to impress upon them the urgency of opening those subfiles.

Running up the stairs, she found Jack and Allyson huddled over a pad at the kitchen table. Allyson was drawing a map or floor plan of some kind. "We've figured out a way to get into the research facility," Jack told her. "I went by the facility and got a look at the work schedule. The night guard is still scheduled to work alone, so we've got to do it tonight."

CHAPTER 22

"Hey, come here, check this," Allyson called to them. While Jack went over the planned break-in with Kayla, Allyson had flipped on the TV. Something she was watching had her leaning forward on the futon, riveted.

Jack and Kayla joined her and they, too, were instantly fascinated. They were watching the CNN5 channel, which was all news, twenty-four hours a day.

Kayla was on the screen — but it was the fake Kayla from the billboards. She was as neatly turned out as ever in a bright pink sweater, matching short skirt, and high boots. Her bobbed hair shone and bounced as if she were in a shampoo commercial. Her silver lipstick and matching eye shadow were perfect.

Zekeal Morrelle stood beside her, appearing as handsome and confident as ever. Kayla wondered why he kept the eye patch. Surely Global-1 could have provided him with a new eye. *He probably just likes the way it looks,* she thought disdainfully.

She didn't think about him for long, though. She was more interested in the smiling young woman beside him — her clone, or one of them, anyway. Although identical to her in so many ways, this girl seemed completely different, so conventional and so docile. She was working on the Tattoo Gen Public Murals Program, so she probably had the same artistic ability as Kayla, Kendra, and Kara. Kayla figured the palm-reader clone would have it, too.

Yet despite their sameness, the lives they'd led had made them so different. With a chill, Kayla also remembered the Gene Enhancement/Manipulation Program file. Had GlobalHelix also had a hand in making them different?

Zekeal and the clone were talking to a crowd, though their voices weren't yet audible. The voice-over announcer spoke cheerily, "Tattoo Gen has sent two of its most high-profile and popular spokespeople on a cross-country book tour to promote their new book, *The Bar Code Way to Happiness*. In it, Zekeal Morrelle tells the fascinating story of his time as an undercover agent for Tattoo Gen. But what is perhaps most appealing here is the emergence of a love story between Zekeal and bar code resister Kayla Marie Reed. Kayla was fleeing police and headed to the Adirondack Mountains to join other resisters when Zekeal went in search of her and convinced her to come home and get the bar code tattoo."

Kayla once again was struck with the eerie sensation that she was looking at what her own life could have been if it had taken an alternate path. It was true that Zekeal had come to the mountains to try to persuade her to return with him and get the bar code tattoo. But in real life, she had refused. She'd run and hid from him until he gave up trying to find her.

What she was seeing now was what would have happened if she *had* given in to him.

"I wonder if that girl even knows she's a clone," Jack said.

"She knows," Kayla replied. "She talks about things that happened to me, not to her. Tattoo Gen has recruited her to play this part."

The voice-over stopped and the camera closed in on Zekeal and the fake Kayla Marie Reed. Zekeal began promoting the book as a biography and as a guide to achieving a sense of belonging in society by being bar-coded.

The reporters in the audience began to ask questions. Zekeal answered them all smoothly until someone addressed one to the fake Kayla: "Kayla, do you feel you were wrong to give up your principles for love?"

"What's she going to say to that?" Allyson asked. She clicked the RECORD button on the remote. "I'm saving this," she said.

"I don't . . . uh, that's not what I did. I . . ." Fake Kayla rubbed her eye, which appeared to be irritated. Flustered, she looked to Zekeal for help.

"She didn't give up her principles. I simply helped her clarify what —"

"Let *her* talk!" someone from the audience shouted.

Fake Kayla began rubbing the other eye with her knuckles.

"She's crying," Kayla said.

With red eyes, the Kayla clone turned to Zekeal. "I can't do this anymore," she said, a sob in her voice. "It's a lie, and I won't have anything more to do with it."

Zekeal realized the microphones were picking up her words. "She's overwrought. It's been a tiring tour," he tried to cover.

"No!" fake Kayla cried. "I want to tell the truth."

Zekeal looked sharply at someone off camera and the screen instantly went blank. In a second, the broadcast was back in the news studio with the anchorwoman. David Young's face appeared on the screen behind her.

"In other news, Decode leader David Young remains on suicide watch. He has refused to take the Propeace prescribed for him. He also continues to refuse to leave his jail cell until the last of the hundred protesters still being held in jail have been freed. Global-1 doctors feel that the incarceration is exacerbating Senator Young's condition and urge him to leave.

"Ambrose Young, father of David Young, obtained a court order enabling him to have a webcam installed in his son's cell. 'I want to make sure those bastards at Global-1 don't hurt my son when no one is looking. I or one of my lawyers will now be looking every second.'"

Allyson turned off the TV, and the three of them sat, stunned. Things were getting even more out of control.

They had to do something about it.

They activated their plan later that night.

It started with Allyson banging on the soda machine in the lobby of the bio/infometrics building where she did her research. "My bar code won't scan on this stupid thing!" she complained loudly. She kicked the machine again.

"Hang on there," the guard at the front desk warned sternly. "Calm down."

"I won't calm down. I just want some damn soda!" she said, dealing the machine another violent blow. "What good is a bar code tattoo if it doesn't even work on a soda machine?"

"The machine was working before," the guard said, coming over to inspect it. "Are you sure you have sufficient funds in your account?"

While Allyson distracted the guard, Kayla and Jack darted past the momentarily abandoned front desk. They took the emergency stairs to the third floor so that the guard wouldn't notice any activity in the elevator. Once there, they ran to unlock the window that led onto a fire escape at the back of the building. A few minutes later, Allyson climbed in through that window, breathing heavily from the exertion. "I'm going to start exercising," she vowed.

Once she had recovered, she unlocked the facility but didn't dare turn on the light. Using a flashlight, she loaded the e-chip into the infometric computer that had been handling related files. She took the second chip, which she'd taped to the underside of a desk drawer, and fed it, too, into the computer. "Come on, Helen," she urged it. "Show us what kind of super hacking beauty you really are. Launch a thousand ships for us."

The computer ran through the first half of the program before it came to the subfiles. Then it began to whir, a sound that made Kayla uneasy. Was something going wrong?

"It's trying alternate ways in," Allyson explained, although she, too, seemed concerned. "It'll keep trying until it finds the one that works."

A silky, feminine robotic voice made Kayla jump and yelp in surprise. "Retinal recognition required," the computer's audio speaker reported. "Provide scan."

Allyson cursed, throwing her arms out in frustration.

"These computers are sucking in info from everywhere, right?" Jack checked with Allyson.

"Right," she confirmed.

"It must be indexing it somehow. How do I access its search engine?" Allyson directed him to a notebook-size unit on a nearby table. It took him close to a half hour, but finally, he stepped back from the computer and smiled. "I am so good!" he boasted. "Jack the hack, that's me."

"What did you do?" Allyson asked.

"I merely searched until I found the GlobalHelix file of employees with computer file clearance. Then I cross-referenced it with their personnel files and broke into them to get coded copies of their eye scans, which, interestingly, are recorded in bar code form. I sent this info over to our infometric friend, Helen of Troy. With any luck she should be getting it any second now."

As if Helen of Troy was acting on his command, a printer buzzed to life, rapidly sending out page after page of material.

Even female computers can't resist him, Kayla thought, smiling inwardly.

Allyson began collecting the papers, reading them with darting eye movements. A crease in her brow deepened as she went. "I don't believe it," she murmured, looking up from her stack of papers. "Take a look at this."

HIGHLY CLASSIFIED
GlobalHelix Population Behavior Control by Nanotechnology

Purpose:

The purpose of the GlobalHelix Population Behavior Control by Nanotechnology program is threefold:

1. To create an orderly global community free of illness and dissent.
2. To rid the world of those individuals promoting illness and/or dissent and create the necessary serving class of the genetically inferior.
3. To identify the mentally and physically strong so as to create a community of cloned persons healthy enough to be involved in the next phase for a planned posthuman future free of disease, aging, and even death, a future of genetically enhanced humans.

See ancillary material below to learn about preliminary trials.

The Program

- Propeace12 Release

Nanomachinery will be capable of a steady, timed release of this amplified version of Propeace. The maximized serotonin-reuptake pharmaceutical can keep patients in a tranquil state indefinitely with few side effects. The most common side effect is kerato-conjunctivitis sicca. This application is recommended for patients with dissident or rebellious tendencies, as indicated in their bar codes, who have not actively engaged in antisocial behavior. It effectively precludes these activities from being initiated by the patient.

- Vagus Nerve Stimulator Release

Nanomachinery will be able to overstimulate the vagus nerve, which has wide connections throughout the brain, with timed electric pulses, thereby inducing a severely depressive state in the patient. At certain low levels this stimulation can offer relief of depression, but at higher levels of activation it creates anxiety and agitation. Patients in this state lack initiative and are rendered inactive. Reported side effects include a constricting pain in the back of the throat, hoarseness, and other odd inflections to the voice. A quiver in pronouncing the *l* sound has been particularly noted in patients speaking Romance- and Germanic-based languages. In some case studies the patient was rendered unable to speak at all.

This application is recommended to patients who are in direct and open rebellion against government directives. Failure to willingly comply with bar code tattoo legislation 16661 constitutes such an infraction of the law and warrants this penalty. Algorithm required for release — highest classification.

- Vagus Nerve Stimulator Intensified Release

Certain patients have been shown to be resistant to the course of treatment indicated above, persisting in their antisocial behavior. In this event, intensification is recommended, with an amplified and more frequent pulse. In 90 percent of cases, suicidal tendencies arise. Without adequate intervention, an attempt will be made. (See below for data on preliminary trial cases.)

- BC12 Virus Release

Nanomachinery is able to mimic known viruses. The bar code 12 virus (BC12) has been developed as a fail-safe in the event that the population behavior control methods described above incur unwanted notice. A change of algorithm is all that is required to switch from vagus nerve stimulation to virus release. Algorithm required — highest classification.

Conclusion

The bar code tattoo program has been highly effective. During the extraction of the mandatory blood sample, self-replicating nanotechnology was injected into the bloodstreams of persons receiving the bar code tattoo.

These molecular-size computers can be activated by codes generated from the central GlobalHelix computer. Each of the strategies discussed above is activated by its own algorithm. By associating the genetic maps recorded in the bar code tattoo with specific algorithms targeted at corresponding individuals, each citizen can be controlled in accordance with his or her exhibited behaviors. A Global-1 caseworker will monitor the movements of approximately 100 patients each. Recommendations will be made on a biannual basis as to which algorithm will be activated in each case.

Ancillary Materials

- Program Activation Dates

Phase I: Trial period. Selected experimental subjects only. Begins September 1, 2024.
Phase II: Forcibly tattooed subjects only. Political and criminal prisoners. Begins October 15, 2025.
Phase III: General population behavior activation. Pending success of phases I and II. Projected start date: January 1, 2026.
For more information on early trial results, see files entitled:

- Genetic Enhancement/Manipulation Program: Donor Kathryn Marie Reed
- Production of Identical Sextuplet Humans During the First Cell Cycle of Nuclear DNA Transfer

- (Subfile) Offspring of Kathryn Marie Reed:
    1. As involved in Population Behavior Control Program (JR-1)
    2. As involved in Genetic Enhancement/ Manipulation Program (KM-1-6)

CHAPTER 23

Allyson swore softly under her breath.

"It's the missing piece," Jack said, stunned by what he'd just read. He leaned heavily on a metal table as though the information had nearly knocked him down. "This has to be what Gene Drake found. He had a friend who was a technology guy for Global-1. He must have had the info file password. If the guy was deep enough inside, he probably had retinal scan clearance, too."

Jack looked sharply to Allyson. "It says the algorithms for these programs have the highest classification. Can Helen of Troy get at them?"

Allyson sighed, uncertain. "I'm not really sure how I would direct it to."

Kayla heard them, but it was as if they were speaking from somewhere far away. She was preoccupied with running the information she'd just read through a mental filter of what she'd experienced in the past year.

It threw everything into a new and clarifying light.

Her parents had been tattooed with their bar codes in September 2024, the period of the trial experiments. Within two weeks, her father had started acting anxious and depressed. He'd stopped going to work and just sat in their den, staring. Before that he'd been energetic, a man who loved books, photography, his wife, and his daughter. Seven months later, he'd killed himself. Her telepathy had been working even then, because some strange feeling had urged her to cut school and hurry home. She'd arrived in time to see the paramedics carry him out on a stretcher.

Now she understood. In the end, they'd gone to their third step with him. They'd amplified the vagus nerve stimulation to the point where he became suicidal.

Kayla vividly recalled the day her father was carried away in the ambulance. Wailing hysterically, her mother had shouted, "The bar code did this to him!"

She'd begged her mother to explain what she'd meant, but she wouldn't. How much had her mother known?

After that, her mother had become like a zombie, drinking alcohol and taking Propeace by the handfuls. Were the nanobots pumping her with Propeace12? Were they zapping *her* vagus nerve with electrical shocks?

Did the GlobalHelix people think she'd become a threat, or was she just part of their experiment? Was her drinking and pill-popping a desperate attempt to fight them, to stabilize her emotions, focus her thoughts, find some tranquillity? In the end she'd tried to burn off her tattoo and killed herself in the fire she unwittingly caused.

Maybe it hadn't been an accident. It might even have been her way to commit suicide, a rebellious conflagration that could have taken down the entire block. She'd known Kayla was in the house. Had she meant to take her, too?

Kayla stopped and pictured her mother as she'd once been, strong and positive.

"Kayla, what are you thinking?" Allyson's voice broke into her recollection. "You're so far away."

"I was thinking about my parents," she revealed. "They must have been involved in the test trial somehow. Before we go we have to get into those other files, the ones about the offspring of Kathryn Reed."

A flashlight beam swung into the facility and the three of them ducked. The guard swept the light across the room as they bent lower, pulling in tight, trying to make themselves as small and inconspicuous as possible.

"We should get out of here," Allyson whispered nervously when he'd moved on.

"I don't know if I can find that eye scan information again," Jack pointed out. "After tonight they might be able to detect that someone was in their files and add even more security. They could even destroy the files. We should get into the files we want to see now, while we still can. We should also copy and print as much as we can."

Allyson glanced anxiously out to the hall. "I don't know."

"I have to look into those files," Kayla insisted.

Allyson gave in. "Let's do it fast," she said.

They first opened one file, then the next two. Together they read them through. Taken all together, they told a compelling story.

Kathryn Marie Reed had been a single mother in 1983 living in the Santa Monica area with her four-year-old son, Joey. Joey's father had left them just before Joey was born, leaving no forwarding address.

Kathryn eked out a living doing portraits for tourists down on the bustling Santa Monica pier. Then one day Joey became listless. He continued to be fatigued and grew paler.

Kathryn had no insurance and no money to pay a pediatrician. A woman who sold tie-dyed shirts on the pier told her that she could sell her eggs to a biotech company in Pasadena. It was called AgroGlobal, and it had recently expanded into genetic research. They shipped the frozen eggs to their laboratories in Korea where scientists could work without the same government restrictions as in the United States.

Desperate, Kathryn Reed went to AgroGlobal and was paid for her eggs. She befriended several doctors there who agreed to look at Joey. They discovered that Joey had leukemia, a disease Kathryn knew had occurred on his missing father's side of the family.

The doctors treated Joey well. Kathryn paid what she could toward this care by participating in more scientific studies.

Joey Reed was eventually cured of his leukemia, but life as an experimental subject had become familiar and comfortable for his mother. With no family other than Joey, it was clear to Kayla that Kathryn Reed had found a place in which she felt at home, and the staff provided the family she'd never had. She apparently liked it at AgroGlobal and stayed on, living full-time at their psychiatric facility in Los Angeles, even when it became GlobalHelix.

Joey Reed was raised in the biotech complex. There he met a young nurse named Ashley McGraw. They were married right on the grounds.

One day in early 2007, Kathryn came to her son with a proposal. She had just been told that one strand of her DNA had been successfully replicated and implanted six times. Sextuplet clones of Kathryn Reed had been produced.

Joey Reed was impressed but not very surprised. He knew advanced human cloning experiments were being conducted by GlobalHelix. These were not the first successful human clones, although they *were* the first six-way split.

But there was more to it. These clones were destined to be the first in an experiment with transspecies gene splicing. Heretofore, animals had been spliced with human genes, but a human had never received an animal gene, at least not on the scale of this experiment.

Which animal's genes would be used?

Not a pig's or an ape's as one might expect. The animal was not even a mammal, but a common sparrow's.

In this case they were not trying to instill a certain trait. Instead, it was a way to discover what traits would emerge. The DNA of each cloned embryo would be injected with increased amounts of avian DNA from a sparrow.

Kathryn asked Joe if Ashley would agree to be the host mother for one of the clones. She'd make sure he got the first clone, the one with the smallest amount of bird DNA. Ashley was experiencing problems conceiving a child, anyway, and this way they could have a child who was genetically from Joe's side of the family. Plus, there would be a large financial reward for this service.

And so Kayla Marie was born to Joe and Ashley Reed on April 16, 2008, a baby girl with avian DNA spliced into the DNA of Kathryn Marie Reed.

Across the country, five other baby girls were also born with these bird genes. A new transgenic creature had come into the world, an avian-human hybrid female.

How would they look?

How would they behave?

Would all six of them be the same? Or would the genes express themselves differently in the six girls?

These things remained to be seen.

It quickly became apparent that GlobalHelix's careful planning — their agenda for monitoring the girls as they grew and developed — was not as foolproof as they had expected.

The surrogate parents reacted in unexpected ways. Some of them were repelled by the offspring in their care. Kara's mother, a young girl who'd been abandoned herself as a baby, sent Kara directly into foster care.

Kayla's parents were suddenly seized with the overpowering urge to protect her from the prying eyes and the control of GlobalHelix. They moved across the country and settled in Yorktown, an upstate New York town still somewhat off the beaten track.

Kendra's parents, too, became highly protective, though their concern for their daughter veered into an obsessive paranoia.

Then came the bar code tattoo. GlobalHelix saw it as their chance to pull in the clones they'd lost track of. As soon as the clones turned seventeen, they'd be bar-coded, and GlobalHelix would know where they were. Then it would be easy to bring them back for further examination and experimentation.

GlobalHelix would be able to do away with them if they proved to be failed experiments — just as they would be able to eliminate anyone who proved inconvenient.

Like everyone else who was tattooed, Joe Reed and Ashley Reed were injected with nanobots when they received their bar codes. Their injected nano-biotechnology was activated, while the nanobots in most of the population sat dormant. They became unwitting participants in the first Population Behavior Control Trial Tests. All the other parents who'd hosted one of the sextuplet clones had been activated, too.

They knew too much.

"The guard is coming again. Get down," Allyson alerted Kayla and Jack urgently as a flashlight beam once again swept the room. Lying flat on the floor, they continued to read the printout rapidly.

Kayla learned the name of the palm-reader clone. Kass Clark. Like Kara, she'd run away from a foster home. Her whereabouts were unknown, but she'd last been seen in the Santa Monica area.

The mystery of her fake, the one on the bill-boards and on TV, was also unraveled. Karinda Carrington was raised on a horse ranch in Virginia by wealthy parents, both of them lead lawyers on the Global-1 legal team. When Karinda had run away from home just before her seventeenth birth-day, they'd hired undercover agents to find her and drag her back. For her seventeenth birthday, she'd been confined to a private sanitarium where she'd been treated by Global-1 psychiatrists and given the bar code tattoo.

And there *was* a sixth clone. KM-6.

Stillborn.

Kendra had been right.

CHAPTER 24

By three in the morning they were back at Allyson's kitchen table feeling overwhelmed by what they'd discovered. "This is so hard to believe," Kayla said. "Is something like this really possible?"

"It's very possible," Allyson confirmed. "Self-replicating nanobots have been around for more than twenty-five years. Only a few of them have to be introduced into the bloodstream, and soon they'll replicate on their own. They're programmed to do that. They can be programmed to fight disease, or they can be programmed to make you kill yourself, apparently." She shivered. "And they're inside all of us with the code."

"Do you think they used suicide nanobots on August?" Kayla asked.

"I'm almost certain they did," Allyson replied. "He was a known bar code resister. Zekeal spotted him in the Adirondacks during a raid and reported him." She swore passionately under her breath, calling Zekeal foul names.

"But he didn't have a bar code," Jack remarked.

"He did," Allyson told him. "He burned it off, but the nanobots were still in his blood. He worked at a biotech plant where he'd witnessed some experiments they didn't want him to see. They threatened him."

"I remember," Kayla said. "They told him that if he didn't live there as a caretaker they'd alter the information in his bar code so he could never get another job. They wanted to make him into a slave. I wonder if the company was a division of GlobalHelix."

"Every biotech company is owned by Global-1, either directly or indirectly," Jack reminded her. "Poor guy. How did he get away?"

"He burned off his bar code tattoo and went into hiding, but I guess they got to him in the end," Allyson concluded grimly.

"This is why David Young is on suicide watch, too," Jack realized. "Remember he said he couldn't talk? That's one of the side effects of that nerve overstimulation thing! I bet they plan to kill him, too. They're just announcing that he's suicidal so no one will suspect. Then they'll zap him with that stimulator when they're ready to get rid of him."

"Oh, I hope not," Allyson said. "But it sure seems like what they have in mind."

"Mfumbe was bar-coded in the roundup," Kayla said, the stunning reality of the situation hitting her with full force. "And now he's so sick and depressed. I was able to make telepathic contact with him and I sensed it."

Her eyes welled with tears that she fought down.

It wasn't a time to be emotional. It was a time to think clearly. They'd beaten him, but he was also very depressed. She was sure he'd already had his nanobots activated with the depression-causing vagus nerve overstimulation. He was a known bar code resister. Did it mean they were going to put him into phase III? Were they planning to kill him?

Allyson got up and took a large manila envelope from a desk drawer. She slipped the thick packet of papers into it. "Tomorrow I'm going to campus early," she told them. "There's a lot of underground Global-1 resistance at Caltech. There's a guy in the infometrics department who does a weekly drop and pickup with a Postman. I want to make a copy of this stuff and get it to Ambrose Young. Are you guys all right with that?"

"It's a good idea," Jack agreed as Kayla nodded. "And after that, maybe we should go to Santa Monica to look for KM-4, Kass Clark."

"I love it here," Kayla said the next day as they walked down the Santa Monica pier boardwalk. A couple on Rollerblades weaved around them at breakneck speed. To the side, a street performer contorted his muscles like a rubber band before landing in a full split.

A very dark-skinned young guy on roller skates whizzed past, thrusting a flyer into Jack's hands as he went. He continued on, passing out the flyers to everyone he passed. "'David Jung and the Fortune

Cookie,'" Jack read, glancing down at it. "Hey, this is written by your friend Mfumbe."

DAVID JUNG AND THE FORTUNE COOKIE

Today, a great champion of the people, David Young, lies in a correction facility hospital bed in a state of deep depression. I believe this depressive state has no organic cause. I believe that David Young has been fed some kind of drug or been immobilized by his enemies in some other way.

In my research I came upon a story of another group of people who, over a hundred years ago, had reason to feel despair about their lives, just as so many of us do today. As we have been encouraged by David Young, so were these people made hopeful by a man with an incredibly similar name — David Jung.

Many scholars believe that the fortune cookie was invented in 1918 by a man named David Jung, a Chinese immigrant living in Los Angeles. David Jung was the founder of the Hong Kong Noodle Company. Concerned about the poor he saw wandering near his shop, he created the cookies and passed them out free on the streets. Each cookie contained a strip of paper with an inspirational Bible scripture on it, chosen for Jung by a Presbyterian minister. Mr. Jung held out a message of hope to the discouraged, just as our

Senator Young has held out hope to all of us by his tireless work and leadership in Decode.

Now it is time for all of us who have benefited from David Young's work to return the favor. Send him messages of hope and encouragement. Write signs and stand below his window with them. Send him inspirational messages inside fortune cookies.

Written by Mfumbe Taylor
Decode member and supporter of David Young

"He's so down and sick himself, yet he managed to get this campaign going," Allyson commented when the three of them had read the paper.

"He must be an amazing guy," Jack remarked.

"He is," Kayla agreed quietly, thinking of him. Did this mean he was feeling better, or had he done it by an extreme effort of will?

They continued walking down the boardwalk, taking in the carnival-like atmosphere. Stationed outside a gigantic old roller-coaster a skinny, barefoot portrait artist with a shaved head sat in a sleeveless undershirt and shorts in front of an easel where he did pastel sketches for twenty dollars. Jack, Allyson, and Kayla stopped to watch him draw a young blond woman wearing only a bikini and Rollerblades.

He was good, working with intense concentration as his hands flew across the paper. Kayla was so involved with watching him work that it took her a minute to realize she knew him. "Artie?" she said.

He looked up at her, annoyed to have his focus diverted, but his expression instantly became friendly. "Kayla! No way!" He held up one finger, indicating that he'd be with her as soon as he'd finished the sketch.

Jack and Allyson stared at Kayla questioningly. "I used to work for him after school at Artie's Art Supply," she explained. "He was the only one who would hire me even though I didn't have a bar code because he didn't have one, either." A quick glance told her he still didn't. "Then one day I showed up at work and the store was locked. His apartment above the store was empty, too."

Artie tore off the sketch and gave it to his pleased customer, who handed over two green marbles. He stood and hugged Kayla warmly. "Why did you leave so suddenly?" she asked. It was a question she'd been dying to ask but never thought she'd have the chance to.

His face clouded over with the unpleasant memory. "You know I have two little girls, right?"

"I know." Kayla recalled the two preschool-aged blond daughters who accompanied their mother through the store on their way up to the apartment every afternoon.

"Social services called us one day after the bar code became law. The woman there said that it had been brought to their attention that my wife, Sally, and I didn't have bar codes . . . which made us unfit parents. It was either get a bar code, pronto, or the girls would be taken away from us. So we ran. Left it all behind and headed across country."

"What bastards," Allyson hissed.

"It was for the best," Artie said. "It's easier to live off the grid out here. I do pretty well at the portraiture — and it's cash money."

"What do you mean, cash?" Jack asked.

Artie smiled at him. "Not cash like it was before they got rid of it in 2020." He held out the two green marbles the woman had just given him. They were engraved with the initials GD.

Opening a metal cash box, he dropped them in among other marbles of various colors. "Each color is worth a different amount. A lot of people live off the grid around here, so we use these as a kind of currency. The Drakians manufacture them and started the whole system. The GD stands for Gene Drake. He was a guy who actually lived near us —"

"We know," Kayla cut him off. "He was my neighbor, and Jack here is a Drakian."

Artie hugged him, unembarrassed. "Keep up the fight, man," he said. "You guys help us all stay strong."

"We do what we have to," Jack replied.

Artie looked at their wrists. "Fakes?" he surmised.

They nodded. "Mine's real," Allyson admitted. "I had to get it in order to go to school."

"No shame," Artie said kindly. "They try to corner us in any way they can. Drakians dropped off a batch of fakes just the other day. I keep a couple for emergencies, but I like to make a little show of resistance by not wearing one."

Kayla told him how her fake contained the file of Kathryn Reed. She said Kathryn was her grandmother, not wanting to go into the whole explanation. "She once did portraits down here, too," she added.

"That's a coincidence," Artie remarked. He opened his cash box and scooped up a handful of marbles. "Take these," he said as he pressed them in Kayla's hand. "I never gave you your last paycheck, and you'll need them around here."

"Thanks."

"You know what else? One day I was positive I saw you here," he said, suddenly seeming to remember the event. "I even ran after you — but it wasn't you. Turns out there's a gal on the boardwalk who reads palms. She could be your twin."

Kayla's heart quickened with excitement. "Do you know where I can find her?"

Artie put a BACK IN FIVE sign over his easel. "I'll take you there."

"I feel I should see her alone," Kayla said after Artie had left them outside a narrow white storefront with a sign saying PALM READER over the door.

"What if she's like Kendra?" Jack worried.

"I'll scream. So don't go too far."

"Be careful," Allyson cautioned.

With a nod, Kayla pushed open the front door. Inside was a very narrow waiting room with three metal folding chairs. A doorway covered with a purple Indian print curtain led into the next room. A sign above the door gave the instruction: READING 25.00 GD. NO BAR CODES ACCEPTED. WAIT TO BE CALLED.

Charcoal sketches of landscapes were tacked to the dirty white wall. Their perspective was from above, as if the artist had been airborne. They were initialed KMC.

Is she dreaming the dreams birds dream, seeing what they see? Kayla wondered.

A young man dressed in surfer trunks and a T-shirt emerged from the back room looking ashen despite his golden tan. "Too freaky," he said when he noticed Kayla.

"Accurate?" Kayla asked.

"I don't know. I hope not, but I guess I'll find out."

"Enter!" a female voice commanded from beyond the curtain.

Kayla walked into a nearly black room. Only the light coming in on either side of the curtain from the outside room allowed her to see the young woman. Her hair was dyed jet-black and bobbed bluntly at the chin. Eyes shut, she swayed back and forth as she sat straight up in a folding chair. Her lip, nose, eyebrow, and ears were pierced with many small silver rings that gleamed in the dim light.

Even in the darkness Kayla could discern her own mouth, nose, chin, and brow.

Kayla sat in the chair that had been placed across from her. "Give me your hand," the palm reader instructed, and Kayla heard her own voice speaking to her.

Kass Clark's eyes remained shut as she stroked Kayla's hand with a hand remarkably like her own. The crashing waves of Venice Beach were the only sound in the room. Kayla remembered the vision she'd had of the two identical hands with the ocean sounds in the background.

Kass abruptly clenched Kayla's hand with great strength. Her eyes snapped open. The eyes beneath the lids were blank, coated with a milky film.

With an involuntary gasp, Kayla realized that Kass was blind.

"You are the other self I have seen in my vision," Kass said, tremendously excited. "It's you. The fire walker."

"Yes. I came here to meet you," Kayla replied.

Kass clasped Kayla's hand in both of hers. "Thank God you're here. In a dream, I have seen a terrible evil. Lines of the living but dead walking into the ocean, robbed of their ability to say no, to resist. Ravaging insects crawl through their blood, setting fires. Their brains are burning! You are the fire-walker self. You have transcended the flame. It's up to you to stop this. Help will be called from the sky, though I do not know if it will come in time to save us all."

Somehow Kayla didn't question her words. She knew what they meant and understood that they were true. Kass was relaying a powerful vision that Kayla trusted. "How can I stop it?" she asked urgently.

"The last self."

"KM-6?"

Kass nodded.

"But she died at birth," Kayla said quietly.

"KM-6 is *not* dead. She went deep inside herself to a place where they would never find her. KM-6 is the phoenix, and I have touched her with my mind. Now you must find her with yours."

CHAPTER 25

Back at Allyson's apartment that night, Kayla lay flat on the futon couch, her eyes shut, thinking, remembering Kass's words. The phoenix — the bird that is burned to ashes but rises to live again.

KM-5, Kendra, had called herself the phoenix, but KM-6 was really the one. She was not dead, only hiding. Hiding someplace where they could never find her.

Allyson came in the front door and crossed the room to Kayla. She sat on the edge of the cushion. "Jack is still at Caltech seeing what he can learn about the Drakians your friend, Artie, said are in the area. I hope he doesn't sneak into the computer room to try to find those algorithms. Helen of Troy can't get them. The codes are too packed with security — but Jack seems hell-bent on trying, anyway."

"It means a lot to him," Kayla remarked. "It means a lot to us all, really."

"Well, it seems hopeless to me," Allyson said. "Anyway, I came back to check on you. Are you okay?"

Kayla turned around to her side, swinging her

legs onto the floor. "Yeah. It was a little upsetting when Kass started screaming at me to go put out the fire." At the end of their talk, Kass had become hysterical, as though the horror of what she saw beyond her blindness was more than she could stand. She stood and demanded that Kayla leave and go do what she had to do. Kayla had backed out of the room, stumbling in the dark, relieved to find Jack and Allyson waiting for her outside.

"I was remembering your other clone, the one pretending to be you," Allyson said. "Did you see the way she kept rubbing her eyes?"

"I figured she was just trying not to cry," Kayla recalled.

"I don't think that was it." Allyson turned on the TV and used the remote to put on the press conference scene that she'd recorded. Zekeal and the fake Kayla stood in front of the crowd. The Kayla clone kept rubbing her eyes. Allyson slowed the action and zoomed in on it. Her eyes were red and irritated but completely dry. "One of the side effects of Propeace12 released by the nanobots is keratoconjunctivitis sicca."

"I remember reading that, but what is it?"

"I looked it up. It's dry eye."

"Dry eye?" Kayla echoed as Allyson's meaning washed over her. "You're saying that she's tranqued up on nanobot-released Propeace12?"

"I'd bet you anything," Alyson said. "The poor

girl probably isn't sure *who* she is, she's so spun around on the stuff."

"Yet we're all so different. Why is Kass the only one who is blind? Why is Kendra so violent?"

"Nature versus nurture," Allyson suggested. "Our genes aren't the only thing that makes us who we are. Our environments and our parents affect us. You were all raised by different people, under different circumstances, in different homes. Maybe there was something in Kass's nutrition or in her home or neighborhood that caused her blindness. Or she could have been in an accident."

"True," Kayla said. "We also have different degrees of transgenic avian genes."

"Not only that," Allyson added. "Genes have multiple tasks. When they began trying to genetically cure sickle cell anemia they discovered that the same gene made people resistant to malaria. By knocking out the disease-causing gene, they could have caused a worse problem. Barbara McClintock proved that genes can even jump around. She won the Nobel Prize for her work with jumping genes. When you start playing around with genes you never really know what will come up."

"It's strange," Kayla said slowly. "The only two of us who are bar-coded — at least that I know of — are Kendra and now Karinda. They were both tattooed against their will. I would have been the third. They were going to tattoo me that night in the hospital after my house burned, but I ran away."

"It's as though you all have a gene for hating the bar code. It's not that strange, I suppose. Studies have shown there's a gene for almost everything," Allyson said. "And besides, you all share a bird's gene. You know the expression 'free as a bird.' A fierce longing to be free might be something GlobalHelix never expected you all to inherit from your little brown sparrow."

"When I was moving your pack, this fell out of it," Allyson said at breakfast the next morning. She handed Kayla the sketch she'd done of Mfumbe the day they walked along the Hudson River. Emotion clutched at Kayla's throat as she looked at it, thinking of his voice reading to her from his slim volume of poetry, *"Come live with me and be my love."*

They'd beaten him up. Were they now going to kill him with nanobots? Would they kill everyone who was at the march . . . or at least everyone they'd managed to catch and bar-code? If it appeared too obvious, perhaps they'd release the BC12 virus instead.

Someone knocked on the door. Kayla assumed it would be Jack, who had once again gone out early to see if he could locate the Drakians. Instead, Allyson opened the door to a clean-cut Asian man Kayla didn't know.

He handed her an underground newspaper. "Your message has been sent with special priority," he said quietly. "The Arts section of the paper is very interesting today. You should check it out."

"Thanks," Allyson said, shutting the door as he left. She went directly to the kitchen table where she opened the paper, shuffling through the pages until she came to the Arts section. There, as she apparently expected, was a letter with the words ALLYSON MINOR, SOMEWHERE IN THE CALTECH AREA, PASADENA, typed on it.

Kayla came to join her at the table. Before she got there, she bent to pick up the splayed National News section that had fallen to the floor. The color photo in the lower righthand corner of the third page immediately grabbed her attention.

Unable to take her eyes from it, she laid it on the table for Allyson to see. The picture showed Kayla — someone looking very much like Kayla — dressed in a long cotton nightgown.

She was on the ledge of a flat-roofed building about to go over the edge.

One bare foot was kicked out in front, and the photo caught the moment when the second delicately arched foot left the ledge. The blond hair and billowy nightgown floated, weightless.

The caption below the photo read: "Kayla Marie Reed leaped yesterday from the top of the Global-1 headquarters in Atlanta, Georgia, in what has been deemed a suicide. This photo was taken with a telephoto ledge from an adjacent building."

Karinda Carrington, KM-3, was dead.

Kayla and Allyson both stared at the incredible photo. "She's trying to fly," Kayla whispered, too moved by this truth to speak any louder.

October 21, 2025

Allyson, hi.

I hope this finds you. I figure the chances are good since a Caltech address is more than Postmen usually have to go on. I hope you're well. I got the news about August through someone from the mountains. I know you two were tight friends. I loved the guy like he was my brother. I feel certain that he didn't do this of his own will. He was too hopeful for that.

I also know because in the last month I have had suicidal thoughts that would never have entered my mind before. Yes, I'm down about a lot of things: I miss Kayla; I'm banged out about what's happening with Dave Young; I feel weak from the beating I took; and having this bar code on my wrist drives me into a murderous rage sometimes.

But despite it all, I love this life too much to ever want to leave it willingly. And yet, lately, I find I can't sleep. My thoughts scatter, and I'm unable to focus. Things that once gave me pleasure, like my cartooning, or poetry, or even peppermint gum, now seem empty, devoid of any ability to satisfy me. It's only through my determination to hang tough and make it through one day at a time that I don't succumb to the darkness that seems bent on engulfing me.

These days this problem does not seem uncommon. Every day the obituary pages of the paper are filled with death notices of more and more people who have committed suicide. Bridges like the Bear Mountain, the Tappan Zee, and all the Manhattan crossings have guards posted now because there has been such a sudden rash of jumpers. No less a figure than David Young remains on suicide watch, so depressed he's unable to utter a word.

But there's hope to be found in the newspapers, too. A lawyer at American Civil Liberties, Nancy Feldman, has noticed that the suicides are predominantly among people who attended the march on Washington in October. She's demanding an explanation. A doctor named Sarah Alan has returned from Canada and is organizing doctors against the bar code tattoo. Her group is called DOC. Coincidentally, she's the daughter of the couple who died in the crash while giving Kayla a ride on the Superlink earlier this year.

Speaking of Kayla, she's my second reason for writing you. I don't know where she is, and I figure she might have headed to you. If you see her, please tell her that I have left my parents' home. If I'd stayed, I really would have killed myself. The medicine they were putting in my food was making me muddleheaded. At least my injuries don't seem too bad anymore.

I got a ride with a friend up the Superlink to the community of bar code resisters in the woods where Kayla and I stayed a while. It was a good move because I have friends there and they've been very kind to me. Also the people here, once content to live in seclusion simply avoiding the bar code, have found it increasingly intrusive in their lives since they all have extended family members and friends who have been affected by it. Consequently, they have an increased willingness to fight back. I believe these pockets exist all over the country and that they are all experiencing the same thing. (I've heard that such a community exists not far from you in the Santa Monica area.)

Tell Kayla, if you see her, not to give in. A lot of information comes and goes out of these woods nowadays. People suspect that something in the bar code has the potential to turn deadly on you. There is no proof, but the rumble of suspicion is out there. And you, Allyson, since you have the bar code, you should lie low. It seems that your bar code hasn't caused you any trouble so far. As long as you don't cause trouble, you'll be okay. But if anyone sees you with Kayla — or a Drakian named Dusa, if she's still with Kayla — well, just be careful.

I won't be easy to find for a while. A group of us are going to Washington to rally around the jail where Dave Young is in the hospital wing. The webcam in his room is active all the time and we're always going to have someone stationed there making sure he doesn't harm himself.

I say I'm going but I'm not sure I can make it. Every day this depression really makes everything difficult. I imagine Kayla has abandoned me. I think all this is really hopeless and — never mind.

Tell Kayla I love her and that I always remember the way she saved that bird the day we left the Adirondacks. She's stronger — and kinder and braver — than she realizes. If you can, please give her the piece of gum I've taped to this page. She'll know what it means. Thanks.

Your true friend always,

Mfumbe

PART 4

Blackbird singing in the dead of night
Take these sunken eyes and learn to see

"Blackbird"
John Lennon and Paul McCartney

CHAPTER 26

Kayla stood in the shower, letting the water drum down on her back. Outside, in the yard below the bathroom window, Jack was showing Allyson the swing-lo's controls. In her mind, she kept going over the words of Mfumbe's letter. It infuriated her to think that Global-1 was wreaking havoc with his emotions and his health with their filthy little nanobots. The miniature technology could do so much good. Leave it to Global-1 to harness its destructive power.

Turning, she positioned her body so that the warm spray could massage her shoulders. A shard of brilliant sunlight found its way past the shade and shower curtain to plant a square of yellow on the white tile wall. Water dripping from the shower gleamed with prismatic beauty in the square, capturing Kayla's attention. It was so magical, each rivulet of water containing a rainbow. She stared at the dripping ribbon of color and let its hypnotic effect carry her off. . . .

* * *

She sees herself standing on a high, twisted ladder mounted on the walled perimeter of a large rectangular rooftop. The person she sees is herself, only very different. Waist-length hair is hopelessly knotted, snarled as though it has never known the stroke of a brush. Some sort of shapeless smock flaps on a scrawny frame. She seems to scan the vivid blue sky with strangely bright eyes.

All the while, she whistles.

The heartbreakingly poignant whistled aria is rich with variety, melodic notes both high and low, some sharp and others sustained for a dramatic, impossible length. And as she whistles into the sky, the face of the whistler is suffused with an inner light emanating from some deep, boundless joy.

The sky darkens ominously as though clouds are amassing at an unnaturally swift pace. A wind begins to beat furiously on the whistling figure, and still she whistles ever louder, as if calling the darkening clouds to her.

* * *

Kayla's eyes opened abruptly and she stumbled back against the tile wall. KM-6! Who else could it be? What Kass had told her was true — KM-6 really *was* alive!

* * *

"What could you see from the rooftop?" Jack pressed her later that afternoon when she told her friends about the vision.

Kayla wasn't sure. She'd been watching KM-6.

"Think," Allyson urged gently. "It might help us find KM-6."

Kayla closed her eyes and concentrated, rebuilding the scene in her mind. "There were mountains," she recalled. "In fact, the building was at the base of a mountain. In the distance, I could see . . . I think I could see Pasadena."

"Okay, so it was close," Allyson surmised. "Anything else?"

"Yes!" Kayla realized. "She was standing on a big metal ladder on the roof. It was huge. And twisted."

"A double helix!" Jack shouted. "The form of DNA. Allyson, where is GlobalHelix located?"

"Everywhere! They have their psychiatric center in downtown Los Angeles, but their main research and corporate headquarters is right here in the San Gabriel Mountains. And they *do* have a giant metal double helix on the roof of their building. I know exactly where they're located."

"Could KM-6 be living right in the GlobalHelix building?" Kayla questioned incredulously. "Kass said she was hiding."

"It's a huge complex," Allyson told her. "I took a

tour of the whole facility with my genetics class in September. She could be right under their noses and they might never know it."

"I guess we're on our way to visit GlobalHelix," Jack said.

The swing-lo was the most efficient way they could think of to get to the GlobalHelix facility. With it, they could shortcut the freeway and the winding, mountainous roads. Since it only held two comfortably, Allyson agreed to stay behind. She handed Jack and Kayla cell phones with clips on the back that they could attach to their clothing. "I'll be here if you need anything," she said. "If I call you, the phone will vibrate silently."

The swing-lo caused a mild stir among people they passed on their way out of Pasadena. Jack kept it just above the ground so that only when someone glanced down did he or she realize it had no tires and wasn't just some new, high-tech, alternate-fuel-burning vehicle.

The freeway was jammed with traffic, and Kayla suggested flying above it. "I don't want to attract that kind of attention," Jack argued. Instead, he buzzed around the sides of the cars or just below the freeway, managing to bypass hundreds of vehicles.

When they left the freeway, Kayla expected him to fly high and braced for the adventure. But he stayed low. *He's afraid to try it,* she realized as they buzzed along country roads.

Before long, they could see the giant black double helix on top of the GlobalHelix building. It was exactly what she'd seen in her vision, assuring her that they'd come to the right place. When they arrived outside the eight-foot wall surrounding the sprawling facility, Jack's face grew pale. "Here goes," he said in a choked voice.

The swing-lo made a whirring noise as he flipped a switch that sent it straight to the top of the wall.

Kayla laughed with delight. "Final level," she said as they hovered there. Tight-lipped with anxiety, Jack flew it over the wall and landed next to a building. Gleefully, she patted his back. "You did it!"

He nodded, breathing heavily as color returned to his face. "At least we know now she really can gain altitude, even though we didn't go very high." He turned to face her. "Did I ever tell you I'm terrified of heights?"

"Yes, you did," she replied.

"Well, I just discovered that fact hasn't changed."

"Are you okay?"

He sat still for a moment, breathing deeply. "I thought I was going to be sick, but I'm okay."

From behind the seats, they took the white lab coats Allyson had given them and put them on.

Jack had gone online and hacked into their personnel files for a copy of the GlobalHelix ID badge, to which they'd added their own scanned-in photos. "If we hit an eye scan we're toast, but this will get us in the door," he said.

It took the two of them to lean the swing-lo up against the building and behind a bush. From there, they walked around front and in through the glass doors. They made no eye contact with the security guards at the long marble front desk but concentrated on appearing like they belonged there, walking purposefully toward the bank of elevators in the center of the sunny lobby.

Oustide the elevator, they scanned the list of floors and departments. Jack poked her and flared his fingers. Glancing up at the list she saw that the tenth floor, at the top of the building, was where they'd find the department of nanobiotechnology. When the crowded elevator arrived, she knew which button to press.

When they got there, they hurried down the quiet hall until Kayla suddenly stopped short, listening intently to a sound that had come into her head.

I can see you. You can see me if you keep coming closer. I'm waiting for you, sister.

"What's wrong?" Jack asked.

"KM-6 just contacted me telepathically."

"Are you sure it's her?"

"No. But she called me sister. She says she can see me."

"Contact her back," he suggested.

Kayla closed her eyes, concentrating. *Tell me how to find you. I am on the top floor. I just got off the elevator. Where are you?*

"Any reception?" Jack inquired softly.

Kayla didn't want to lose focus and held up her hand for him to wait.

A girlish giggle filled Kayla's mind, followed by a whistled note. *Turnthecornerturnthecornerturnthe corner.* The telepathic words came in a nursery-rhyme singsong.

"She's around the corner." They hurried to the end of the long hall and skidded to a stop as they raced around the doorway to another long corridor.

It was empty. That's what they thought at first, but then they spied a lone figure at the far end, mopping the floor.

Hurrying toward her at first, Kayla slowed as she got closer. The young woman didn't stop mopping or seem to register their presence in any way. A mass of tangled brown hair was held back loosely with a rubber band. She wore an ill-fitting shift with a smock over it. She was skinny, almost painfully so. Kayla couldn't help but think that she probably ate like a . . . bird.

This was KM-6, the clone she'd seen. There was no doubt. But she wasn't what she'd expected.

I'm hiding. You can't see me. It was a child's voice that came into Kayla's mind.

Don't be scared. It's me, your sister, Kayla spoke

telepathically. Her message was received. KM-6 swung her head around to stare straight at Kayla with the wide-open black pupils of a dark-eyed bird.

"She's got some form of autism," Jack realized after repeated attempts to talk to KM-6 failed.

You don't have to talk out loud. We talked mind to mind before. Let's do it again, Kayla tried, contacting KM-6 once more.

KM-6 dropped the mop she'd been clinging to and turned her face to the wall, wrapping her hands over her head.

Kayla's mind was immediately flooded not with words but with pictures. They came to her with rapid-fire, dizzying speed: *A baby living in staff housing facilities, right here in the GlobalHelix complex. Nurses sneak in to feed her, care for her, a succession of different caretakers come and go. The cleaning staff adopts her, caring for her at night. As she grows, they make her a bed in a utility closet. She works with them. This is her home, the only one she's ever known.*

"Why would the nurses and cleaning staff do something like that?" Jack asked when Kayla told him what she'd seen.

"I can't be sure, but I bet I know," Kayla said. Along with the pictures, she'd received emotions from KM-6. She loved the nurses and cleaning staff. She was safe with them. It was the GlobalHelix scientists and doctors she feared. "It seems like she was born right here, maybe in a synthetic womb. She's KM-6 which means she has the most avian DNA in her. They weren't happy with the way she came out — and so they called her stillborn and planned to kill her."

"And some nurses whisked her away, reported her dead, and the staff here secretly raised her," Jack supplied.

A consenting hum in Kayla's mind told her they had gotten it right.

CHAPTER 27

We want to help you, Kayla sent a mind message to KM-6. Abruptly, KM-6 ran down the hall away from Kayla and Jack. "We have to go after her," Kayla said.

Jack shook his head. "I think we'd better find the nanobiotech department first." They continued down a hall until they came to it. Inside, Jack hacked into a file and loaded the information onto a chip he'd brought in.

The round cell phone clipped to Kayla's shirt vibrated and she pressed the center button to answer. "What's happening?" Allyson asked.

Before Kayla could reply, two men in lab coats came into the room, angrily demanding to know why Jack and Kayla were there. "We work here," Kayla bluffed.

"No, you don't. I know everyone who works in this department," one of them barked.

The other pulled a phone from his lab coat pocket. "Security emergency on tenth floor, nanobiotech," he instructed.

"Give me that," the first man demanded, noticing the chip Jack was trying to sneak into his pocket.

Jack's eyes darted around the room, searching for a way out. When nothing occurred to him, he put the chip in his mouth and swallowed.

"Too bad you did that," the second man said. "We were just going to have security escort you and your friend out. Now we can't let you leave."

A dauntingly muscular guard appeared in the doorway. "Keep them here while we go get the department heads," the first man commanded him as they left. Kayla and Jack were alone with the guard, who stood facing them, stone-faced.

What would happen to them now? GlobalHelix wouldn't know how much they had seen, but they'd suspect it was too much. It would be so easy for them to make Jack and Kayla disappear. They'd inject them with nanobots, activate the BC12 virus, and they'd be gone and no one would know they'd been murdered.

Allyson would know. But she had a tattoo, which meant nanobots were in her bloodstream, making her easy to eliminate as well.

Kayla heard a thud and gasped as the security guard staggered forward, blood pouring down the back of his neck.

It took Kayla a second to realize what she was looking at. KM-6 stood in the doorway brandishing a five-foot, iron-bladed, blood-smeared garden shovel.

"Run!" Jack shouted, grabbing Kayla's arm.

The guard was down but he wasn't out. There

wasn't much time before someone else would be alerted.

Kayla beckoned for KM-6 to follow as they raced to the elevator bank. She was with them when they saw two guards coming in their direction. A quick reversal revealed two more guards blocking the hall behind them.

KM-6 lunged for a door in the middle of the hall, and they followed her up a stairway leading to the roof. They heard the guards close at their heels, but KM-6 slammed the door, locking the dead bolt.

"Now we're trapped up here," Jack pointed out.

At almost the same instant a lightweight helicopter loomed up from behind the building. G-1 SECURITY was printed boldly on its side. "Stay where you are," a voice from the helicopter boomed over an address system. "We will be landing. Be advised that we are authorized to carry and use weaponry."

Jack swore. Kayla searched in every direction for an escape as the wind from the descending helicopter whipped up her hair.

KM-6 raced for the huge double helix at the center of the building and began to climb it. Her tangled hair had come free from the rubber band and danced around her face, blown by the helicopter.

She started to whistle.

Kayla was close enough to hear her despite

the noise of the helicopter. It was the same hauntingly plaintive song Kayla had heard in her vision of KM-6.

The sky began to darken. Gazing up, Kayla saw that it was not clouds that were gathering in the sky above her.

It was birds.

A blanket of birds.

KM-6 was calling birds to create a barrier protecting them, making it impossible for the helicopter to land.

They remained on the roof, safe for the moment but not knowing what to do next. On the other side of the door someone began banging. How long would it take before they broke through?

The swing-lo suddenly rose and hovered next to the roof ledge, with Allyson at the controls. "Come on. Let's fly," she shouted.

KM-6 climbed down from the double helix when she saw the craft and joined them at the ledge wall. "Climb in," Kayla urged her. She turned to Jack, who'd climbed in beside Allyson. "Will it hold all of us?"

"Let's hope so," he replied, extending a hand to KM-6 and then to Kayla. The swing-lo dipped precariously under their weight but stabilized.

Allyson sent the swing-lo forward. As they went, the craft slowly lost altitude. "We're not going to make it over the wall," she worried as it loomed into sight.

"It has to," Kayla said. "Look!" Below them, Globalofficers were stationed by the wall. Three cars were parked and various guards were in position.

Allyson pounded at the buttons of the control panel, but the swing-lo continued to descend. The button on the cell phone clipped to her collar vibrated and she answered. "Bad!" she spoke to someone on the other end. "We're about to crash into the inside of the wall by the front gate."

But, amazingly, something prevented that from happening. Security guards were suddenly running for safety as debris and dust flew around them.

A tractor trailer had rammed right through the front wall!

CHAPTER 28

Gunshots were fired as Allyson steered the swing-lo into the open trailer of the truck, sliding in for a landing and avoiding a collision with the cab end by inches.

"Aha!" Kayla exulted, hugging KM-6. "We're birds. We always fly away!" KM-6 hunched her shoulders nervously but didn't pull away from her.

Jack was pale and shocked. He barely noticed as Nate and Francis helped lift him from the swing-lo.

"Final level on the timing!" Kayla praised them. "Where did you guys come from?"

"That's what I called to tell you," Allyson said, climbing out of the swing-lo as the truck sped on. "Those days when Jack went out looking for the Drakians he left messages with Postmen — and you know the Postmen always come through. Nate, Francis, Dusa, and your friend Amber showed up right after you left. I was calling to tell you we were on our way to GlobalHelix in case you needed backup. When those G-1 guys surprised you, you left the line on your phone open and we could hear everything that was going on."

"You know Dusa; when she puts the pedal to

the metal, she gets there fast," Nate said, with a laugh.

"When we arrived, Dusa drove the truck around the facility to the service entrance as if making a delivery. I figured you'd stashed the swing-lo somewhere nearby," Allyson continued. Kayla could figure out the rest. Amber, Dusa, Nate, and Francis had driven back out beyond the wall to wait while Allyson flew the swing-lo to the roof to rescue them.

"How did you know how to fly it?" she asked Allyson.

"Jack showed me the other day in the yard," she replied, smiling proudly.

Jack was slumped against the side of the truck, still ashen. "I hate heights," he muttered.

Kayla went to his side and rubbed his arm affectionately. "You did it, though. You faced your worst fear."

"Yeah, I guess so," he agreed, looking a little happier. "Hey, pal — we did do it, didn't we!"

"It's too bad we won't have access to that chip you swallowed," she said. "At least not for a while."

With a grin, he stuck out his tongue — and peeled off the chip.

After they left Dusa's truck at a parking lot at Caltech, they walked back to Allyson's apartment. Dusa explained that they'd volunteered to come to Santa Monica to drop the tattoo fakes and the GD marbles because they'd also wanted to check on

Jack and Kayla. "We knew you were around Caltech but we didn't know exactly where to find you until a Postman gave us Jack's message. We came over as soon as we got it."

KM-6 walked along with them, listening alertly but saying nothing. She seemed to have lost her fear of them.

As they climbed the steps to the apartment, Dusa explained that before coming to California, she and Amber had driven to Washington, DC, to join the rally around David Young's hospital jail cell. He was no longer on suicide watch but seemed to be dying of some strange virus.

"We know what's really wrong with him," Allyson said, and revealed all they'd learned about the nanobots.

Dusa, Nate, Francis, and Amber were as amazed as Kayla, Jack, and Allyson had first been. "See? Gene knew," Francis remarked sagely.

"The BC12 virus . . . that must be what's wrong with David Young," Amber guessed. "And Mfumbe, too."

Kayla stopped in front of the apartment door. "Mfumbe?"

"We met him at the rally and brought him with us," Dusa said. "He suddenly stopped being depressed, but he's real sick, Kayla."

Kayla was in the living room the moment Allyson unlocked the door. Mfumbe was asleep on the futon and she hurried to his side. His face glistened with sweat. He was much thinner than the last time she'd seen him. "We have to get him to a hospital," she said.

"That wouldn't do any good," Dusa said. "They're all G-1 run, and he's on their list. If G-1 is trying to kill him, they're not going to help him get better."

Jack sat at the kitchen table staring at Allyson's handheld computer screen. He was running the information he'd downloaded from the GlobalHelix computers and tapping his fingers on the table, deep in thought. "Those nanobots are the size of molecules, but they're still robots, which means they're computerized," he said, his eyes still riveted to the screen.

Allyson came and sat beside him. "What are you getting at?"

"If I could find the algorithms that control the nanobots I could shut them down, maybe even make them short-circuit."

"In everyone?" Allyson asked him.

"Well, they're sent to individual bar code identities, but they emanate from a single computer program. If I could shut down that program it should make the nanobots in every identity shut down. But by the time I can figure out the algorithm codes, GlobalHelix will have blocks in place."

A nursery song filled Kayla's head, and she looked sharply to KM-6. Her eyes were closed as she rocked back and forth on a kitchen chair. Closing her own eyes, Kayla listened to the words of the song.

But they weren't words.

KM-6 was singing her a nursery rhyme made up of numbers and letters, brackets, spaces, colons, and backslashes.

Kayla began to shout out what she was hearing, her eyes still closed, still concentrating.

"Algorithms!" she heard Allyson cry.

Jack jumped up as though he'd been shot from his chair, knocking it to the floor. "I don't believe it!" he shouted. "It's the algorithms. She's got the secret algorithms! KM-6 is sending them to her!"

CHAPTER 29

"Somebody get a pad!" Jack shouted, wildly searching for something to write on.

"I don't have a pad!" Allyson said in a panicked voice.

"I'm writing already," Amber shouted as she scribbled on a paper napkin with eyeliner. "I've got it all so far!"

Kayla continued to announce each piece of the algorithm as she received it from KM-6. Her heart pounded but she fought it down, needing to hear clearly what was coming into her head.

She remembered reading about certain types of people with autism who had a special ability to remember nearly unbelievable chains of numbers, dates, addresses, and the like.

KM-6 had grown up in a biotech facility. These were her nursery rhymes.

Finally, KM-6 stopped sending the codes and slumped in her chair. Kayla, too, felt drained of energy.

Jack ran to the computer on the kitchen table, typing in the characters Amber had written on napkins, paper, towels, old envelopes, and even her arm. "I think it's working!" he shouted.

They all stared at him, breathless with anticipation.

"It looks like it's shutting down," he said again, his voice more confident as his certainty grew. "It's working!"

They screamed with joy, hugging one another. Jack grabbed KM-6, swinging her in a circle. The girl didn't seem to mind.

They had done it! They'd used the secret G-1 algorithms to shut down the entire behavior control program! Jack quickly sprang into action and put his own lock on the system so Global-1 couldn't reactivate it.

Kayla glanced at Mfumbe on the futon.

He opened his eyes at the same moment and slowly smiled at her.

DAVID YOUNG LEAVES JAIL A WELL MAN AS LAST PROTESTER IS RELEASED

Washington, DC. November 8, 2025 — In a stunning recovery, David Young left his hospital room early this morning. Upon learning that the last protester arrested during the October 13 protest had been released, he got dressed and walked outside where he was met by the press and a throng of ever-growing supporters. He thanked the crowd for their faith in him and their many letters and cards. He also thanked whoever started the movement to send him fortune cookies with encouraging messages. "They helped me hang on in my darkest moments," he said. "I read every one of them."

He was joined by his father, Ambrose Young. "This is far from over," Ambrose Young told the press.

AMBROSE YOUNG DROPS GLOBAL-1 BOMBSHELL

Washington, DC. November 12, 2025 — Today, Ambrose Young presented evidence to the United States Senate of a shocking plot by the multinational company Global-1 to control the citizens of the United States as well as other nations by the use of embedded nanotechnology. Citing proof from an undisclosed source, former Senator Young turned documents over to the Speaker of the House that detail the company's program. The Global-1 plan has been in the works since the inception of the bar code tattoo. President Loudon Waters is mentioned as the vehicle by which Global-1 intended to implement universal compliance with the bar code. By day's end, sixteen senators had called for impeachment proceedings to begin.

DR. SARAH ALAN HEADS MOVEMENT OF DOCTORS OFFERING FREE LASER TATTOO REMOVAL

New York, NY. November 30, 2025— Dr. Sarah Alan is happy to be back in her office. She is even happier with the new tattoo-removing laser she's purchased. In conjunction with a nationwide network of doctors working with and coordinated by Dr. Alan—Doctors of Compassion (DOC)—bar code tattoos are being removed from morning until late into the night. "Some people still think they're cool and want to keep them," Dr. Alan said. "That's their right, but there's no more information stored in them other than the person's name. As for the embedded nanorobotics, our panel of physicians has studied the issue and released a paper stating that we believe the nanos will disintegrate over a six-month period if they are not utilized. The representative from Global-1 confirmed our findings during last month's Senate investigation."

DAVID YOUNG ANNOUNCES PLANS FOR A PRESIDENTIAL RUN AS AN INDEPENDENT CANDIDATE

Washington, DC. December 31, 2025— David Young announced today that he is throwing his hat in the ring and making a bid for the presidency in the upcoming special election scheduled for this March. Though he has many supporters from both parties, Young says he can be most effective as an Independent. "The many people in this country who have supported me have had enough of self-serving special interest groups," he told the press today. Among his campaign promises, Young has vowed to work with other nations affected by the nanobiotech threat of the bar code tattoo. He also promises a special commission dedicated to addressing and righting wrongs perpetrated on citizens hurt by the bar code tattoos. In addition, he has promised a spate of new legislation aimed at protecting rights of individual privacy. "New technologies will always offer the greedy and power hungry new opportunities to oppress its citizenry. Advances in science must be made with due consideration. They can advance the health and well-being of all people, or they can enslave them. In a free society we must work together to make this a world where human dignity is the yardstick by which we measure progress."

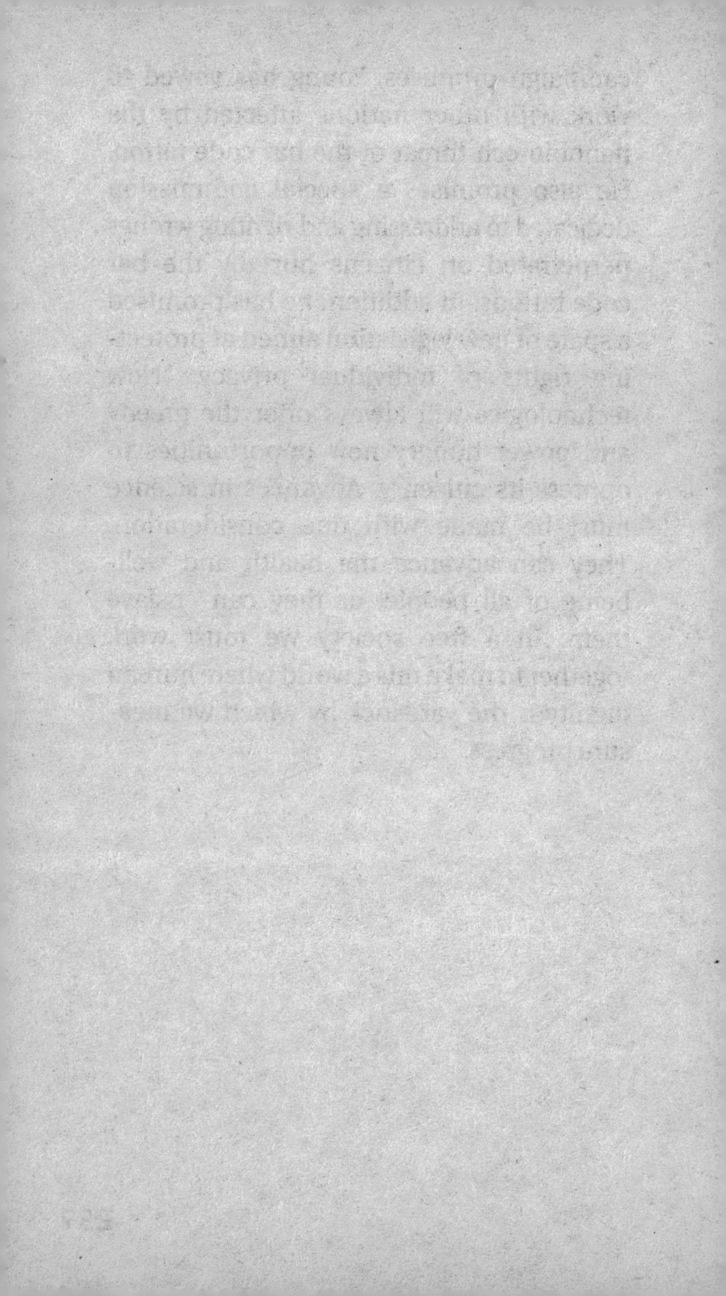

EPILOGUE

It gives me great pleasure
indeed to see the stubbornness of an
incorrigible nonconformist warmly acclaimed.

Albert Einstein

The world, which had been shut down, lost to them, was back. And yet it would never be the same to Kayla.

She had made peace with the idea of being a clone. It was really no stranger than being a twin — or a sextuplet. She wouldn't be the first person on earth to have to deal with *that.*

Being transgenic, part bird, was a bit more complex. What did it mean for her future health? In the last week of December, she phoned Dr. Sarah Alan's office in New York, DOC headquarters. Dr. Alan herself picked up the phone, and when Kayla gave her name she was met with silence on the other end. "Excuse me," the doctor spoke after a moment, "but I thought you were . . . I thought I read in the paper that you . . ."

"I'm not dead," Kayla said. "That wasn't me. It was a clone."

"A clone," Dr. Alan echoed. "My mother phoned and told me all about you before she and Dad died. They were very fond of you. Are you all right?"

"I think so," Kayla said. "But I have serious things I'd like to talk to you about. May I make an appointment for myself and my . . . sister? She's a clone, too."

Kayla didn't feel a compelling responsibility toward Kendra, Kara, or Kass. But KM-6 was different.

KM-6 had saved the world — in a way.

She'd also saved Kayla's life — probably.

KM-6 made Kayla think of the black-capped chickadee she'd brought back to life that day in the Adirondacks. She wondered now if she could do as much for KM-6. She was willing to try, anyway.

"Bring her in to see me," Dr. Alan said. "I'll have a few of my associates available, and we'll figure out what you both need. Make an appointment for sometime in early January."

Dusa came into Allyson's apartment on New Year's Day, a bit weary from the hearty party to bring in 2026 that they'd attended at Artie's place, but ready to make the trip back east as planned. "Now that I don't have to be scary anymore, I'm going back to my real name," she announced. "I'll join the *K* club as an honorary member."

"We don't have a Katie," Kayla said. "Join the club."

KM-6 was sitting by the window, staring out. The long dark hair they'd brushed to a shine for her gleamed in the sunlight. With better clothing and grooming, her resemblance to Kayla was more obvious, but she still seemed frail, birdlike.

"Speaking of the *K* club," Katie said, crossing to KM-6, "you have a family now, kiddo. And I think you need a better name than KM-6. Do you like Karen?"

KM-6 looked up at her. For the first time they'd seen, she smiled.

"Okay!" Katie said, returning the smile. "Karen it is!"

Mfumbe came out of the bathroom and wished everyone a happy new year. From the moment Jack shut down the nanobots, his recovery had been rapid. Occasionally, he felt pain where he'd been injured in the Washington beating, but mostly he was better.

The moment Kayla had seen him again she knew her love for him was as strong as it had ever been. They'd decided to go to Washington, DC, to work on the David Young presidential campaign. After that, Mfumbe wanted to apply to college. He'd once been offered a scholarship he couldn't take because he had no bar code. Now that the bar code was no longer required, maybe the scholarship would still be available.

Kayla didn't know what she'd do. She was still wanted by the police. Mfumbe was, too, for assaulting Zekeal during the raid last summer. But the G-1 police were under intense scrutiny, and she'd heard that cases involving infractions of bar code tattoo policy were being dropped or simply forgotten. She knew they didn't really think she'd burned down her house or been responsible for her mother's death. They had simply wanted a reason to bring her in. It was likely that all the charges against her would simply go away.

They were just about packed and ready to leave when Allyson and Jack came in. "We've made a decision," Allyson announced, beaming with pleasure.

"You're getting married," Katie guessed.

"Worse," Jack told her, also clearly happy. "We're incorporating!"

"What?" Kayla asked.

Allyson sat at the kitchen table. "We talked about it all last night. The swing-lo works. It just needs to be made to look more sleek, more attractive. We want to go into business and be one of the first companies out there with it. We met these guys who invest in startup companies last night at the party, and they're really interested in funding us."

Kayla hugged Allyson. "That's so exciting!"

"When you get big, you might need private trucking to deliver the swing-los," Katie mentioned.

"Absolutely," Jack agreed.

"Kayla, I love your art," Allyson said. "Could you start working on a company logo for us?"

"Sure."

"If this company is a success, we want you to be our art director," Allyson added.

"That would be so final level," Kayla said, excited

at the idea. She immediately envisioned a drawing of the swing-lo flying beside . . . a bird. Maybe a whole flock of birds.

She suddenly remembered the first stanza of a poem Mfumbe had recently read to her from the slim volume of poetry he'd been carrying around. It was called "Hope" and was by Emily Dickinson:

Hope is the thing with feathers
That perches in the soul
And sings the tune without the words
And never stops at all.

For the first time in a year, Kayla saw her possibilities as limitless. And she was filled with new hope.

Go wherever life takes you...

☐	0-439-63616-7	Shadow of the Red Moon	Walter Dean Myers	$5.99 US
☐	0-590-48141-X	Make Lemonade	Virginia Euwer Wolff	$5.99 US
☐	0-590-40943-3	Fallen Angels	Walter Dean Myers	$5.99 US
☐	0-590-31990-6	When She Was Good	Norma Fox Mazer	$5.99 US
☐	0-590-47365-4	Plain City	Virginia Hamilton	$5.99 US
☐	0-590-45881-7	From the Notebooks of Melanin Sun	Jacqueline Woodson	$5.99 US
☐	0-590-48142-8	Toning the Sweep	Angela Johnson	$5.99 US
☐	0-590-42792-X	My Brother Sam is Dead	James Lincoln Collier/ Christopher Collier	$5.99 US
☐	0-590-46715-8	When She Hollers	Cynthia Voigt	$5.99 US
☐	0-439-36850-2	Winter	John Marsden	$5.99 US
☐	0-439-70682-3	Good-bye and Keep Cold	Jenny Davis	$5.99 US
☐	0-439-59851-6	The Haunting of Alaizabel Cray	Chris Wooding	$7.99 US
☐	0-439-55479-9	Singer of All Songs (The Chanters of Tremaris Book 1)	Kate Constable	$5.99 US

Available wherever you buy books, or use this order form.

Scholastic Inc., P.O. Box 7502, Jefferson City, MO 65102

Please send me the books I have checked above. I am enclosing $________ (please add $2.00 to cover shipping and handling). Send check or money order—no cash or C.O.D.s please.

Name________________ Age______

Address________________

City________________ State/Zip________

Please allow four to six weeks for delivery. Offer good in the U.S. only. Sorry, mail orders are not available to residents of Canada. Prices subject to change.

SCHOLASTIC

www.scholastic.com

POINT

PNTBL0806